# WELLS FARGO DECOYS

The Sierra Stash was a twenty-year-old legend, a cached fortune in gold, a prize that triggered greed and homicidal tendencies. Now the secret was out. One person had acquired the Marchmount map, the key to the whereabouts of the cache. The deadly gang led by Reno Hamill closed in for the kill, and where were the Texas Trouble-shooters? Hidden, armed and ready for a running fight.

# MARSHALL GROVER

♦

# WELLS FARGO DECOYS

A Larry & Stretch Western

*Complete and Unabridged*

# LINFORD
*Leicester*

First published in Australia in 1989 by
Horwitz Grahame Pty Limited
Australia

First Linford Edition
published 1996
by arrangement with
Howitz Publications Pty Limited
Australia

British Library CIP Data

Grover, Marshall
    Larry & Stretch: Wells Fargo decoys.
    —Large print ed.—
    Linford western library
    I. Title II. Series
    823 [F]

    ISBN 0–7089–7820–7

Published by
F. A. Thorpe (Publishing) Ltd.
Anstey, Leicestershire

Set by Words & Graphics Ltd.
Anstey, Leicestershire
Printed and bound in Great Britain by
T. J. Press (Padstow) Ltd., Padstow, Cornwall

This book is printed on acid-free paper

# 1

## Another Town, Another Ruckus

**W**OODVILLE 'Stretch' Emerson rose from the swivel chair of the barber shop and admired his reflection in the mirror held by the barber before donning his battered Stetson.

"Right fine haircut, amigo," he remarked. "I never looked better."

The barber grouched. This aptly nicknamed Texan, six and a half feet and built like a beanpole, had the unruliest thatch of tow hair he had ever clipped or combed; a real challenge. He said as much and complained he ought to charge the stranger double.

"Your hair's like wire and it grows every whichaway."

Stretch flashed him a grin, paid him and added a tip. The barber shop was

1

next door to one of the bigger saloons of Porterville, West California, and Red Rose operated by one Al Spencer.

"Better go check on my partner," the taller drifter said in farewell. "By now, he's maybe all caught up in a poker party and losin' our roll."

In good humor, he walked the few yards from the barber shop to the batwings of the Red Rose. 'I never looked better' had been an offhand comment. He was incapable of conceit, and this was fortunate because, in truth, only a liar would call Stretch Emerson handsome. He was, with his long chin, too-wide mouth and jughandle ears, as homely as they come. Rigged in range clothes that had seen better days, he packed a Colt at either hip, and the second .45 was no mere showpiece; with handguns he was ambidextrous.

Entering the crowded bar-room around 2 o'clock this afternoon, he glanced to the area accommodating games of chance. His partner of many years, a brawny Texan only three inches

2

shorter than he, was right where he had anticipated, filling a chair at a poker table, pitting his wits and his poker skill against five locals. Dark-haired with a certain battered handsomeness, Larry Valentine was the thinking half of the nomadic duo known to the law and the lawless as the Lone Star Trouble-Shooters, nimble-witted and, as he grew older, becoming somewhat of a cynic, though his sense of humor was surviving. He traded nods with his partner, who made his way to the bar to order beer.

At poker, Larry was no amateur, an old hand in fact and possessing all the instincts of a veteran gambler. He had, since sitting in on this game, won $60 and dropped $50. Not being the sore loser type, being only $10 ahead caused him no disquiet.

Even so, he was leery of the dapper man seated directly opposite him. Only one player had thought to identify himself to Larry. Alonzo Grade, the townsman seated at his left, was a sallow, surly citizen, the kind he wasn't likely to warm to, but he could ignore Grade, if not the dapper character with the smug grin. That one he watched closely, for cardsharps were one of his aversions and he suspected him to be just that.

He waited till he was certain before taking action. The other players flinched as the grimfaced stranger leaned across the table and, in one deft movement, whisked a card from inside the dapper man's left shirtcuff.

"Like to give yourself an edge, huh?" he growled, exhibiting the ace of clubs. "Hideaway high cards."

"Well, what do you know?" The dapper man grinned unconcernedly. And, to Larry's disgust, nobody else protested; the other players averted their eyes. "It must've slipped in there by accident while I was shuffling."

Larry glowered at him and declared, "To believe that, I'd have to be brainless."

The dapper man, much younger

than Larry but, in Larry's opinion, old enough to know better, yawned boredly and identified himself; he sounded arrogant now.

"I'm Jason Teague."

"Is that supposed to mean somethin' to me?" retorted Larry.

"If you know what's good for you . . . " began Jason Teague.

"I know you're a cheatin' polecat and not the smartest sharper I ever caught out," snapped Larry. "And I'm damned if I savvy why these hombres hold still for it." He challenged the other players. "Whatsamatter? You all blind?"

Impatiently, the sharper snapped his fingers. The bouncer, a bartender and three of Spencer's tablehands promptly responded to what was obviously a summons, converging on Larry. Observing this, Stretch shrugged resignedly and drained his tankard.

"He irritates me, this saddletramp." The dandy gestured contemptuously to Larry. "Throw him out."

At first, Larry couldn't believe it. The saloon-keeper, seated alone at a corner table, appeared downright embarrassed, but refrained from protesting the cardsharp's demand. Then Larry had to believe it, because the faro dealer grasped him by an arm and hauled him from his chair.

Larry reacted by driving the wind out of the faro dealer with a hard left to the solar plexus, and that was just the start of it. Before Spencer's other employees could forestall him, he reached across the table again, seized Jason Teague by his ruffled shirtfront, backhanded him twice, lifted him and hurled him. Yelling, the cheater hurtled through the air. A nearby table was hastily vacated and maybe it was poorly constructed — in any event it collapsed when the human missile struck it.

"Now, gents," Stretch chided, as the other housemen aimed blows at his partner. "Five against one ain't fair."

Nobody was listening. Larry was retaliating in his usual ham-fisted style, but against five attackers, so the taller Texan did what came naturally, bounded into the mêlée, dodged a swing from the roulette man and flattened him with a hay-maker.

Grade and the other players hustled to disassociate themselves from the action. With other patrons, they retreated to what they hoped would be safe vantage-points, the side walls, the staircase, while the hellers from the Lone Star State set about convincing their assailants that their allegiance to a no-good cardsharp was not the best idea they'd ever had. Certainly the bouncer was convinced. Larry's lusty uppercut sent him reeling to the demolished table to crash atop the prone and wailing Jason Teague, pinning him.

Stretch subdued the blackjack dealer with a nose-crushing left while the bartender attempted to grapple with Larry, only to be returned to the place from whence he'd come. Growling ferociously, Larry grasped him by a wrist and an ankle, swung mightily and let go and, like an outsized bird, the dispenser of cheer flew over the bar counter to hit the floor beyond with a resounding thud.

When Deputy Sheriff McElroy arrived to draw and cock his six-gun and demand a cessation of hostilities, it was all over anyway. Adversaries of the Texans still visible were prone, some groaning, some out cold. Pinned down by the weight of the unconscious bouncer, Jason Teague was yelling in agony and demanding medical treatment. The Texans were merely dusting themselves off and aiming cold stares at the deputy's levelled pistol.

"Holy Moses!" breathed McElroy.

"Somebody roll this lummox off me!" cried Jason Teague. "And you, McElroy throw those strangers in jail!"

"That's how it's gonna be?" Larry challenged all and sundry. "The dude sharper says jump, so every sonofagun jumps?"

"Let's have no more trouble here," frowned McElroy. "Unbuckle your sidearms, pass 'em to me slow and careful, then come along peaceable."

"What the hell, runt," shrugged Stretch.

"Yeah," Larry sourly agreed. "What the hell."

With the deputy hefting their coiled shellbelts and filled holsters and unaware he was arresting a couple of living legends, the drifters walked Porterville's main street for three blocks to the county jail and the office of Sheriff Frank Brentnall. Like his deputy, Brentnall showed no inclination to heed the protests of the tall strangers. McElroy repeated the cardsharp's demand they be locked up, and Brentnall grimaced and nodded.

Alonzo Grade entered while McElroy was installing the Texans in a two-bunk cell. Brentnall eyed him warily.

"Now just what the hell do you want, lawyerman?"

"You get their names?" asked Grade,

9

nodding to the jail-house entrance. "I'll need their names, Sheriff. I'm going to represent them."

"Their idea or yours?" demanded Brentnall.

"Mine," grinned Grade, and the grin was spiteful. "I'm sure I can convince them. This was unlawful arrest. Jason Teague ordered Spencer's employees to attack them. And that, Sheriff Brentnall, is not exactly legal either — is it now?"

"You've been waiting your chance," sneered Brentnall.

"Right," Grade said with relish. "Now what are their names?"

"I didn't ask," shrugged Brentnall.

"Of course not," jibed Grade. "Mayor Teague's word is law. His spoiled-rotten son gets exactly what he deserves — for the first time — so these cowboys have to be the patsies." McElroy emerged, picked up the prisoners' sidearms and hung them on the gunrack. "Well? Can you refuse them legal representation, Sheriff? Is the

10

Teague influence *that* powerful?"

"Go talk to 'em," invited Brentnall, "if embarrassing the mayor means that much to you."

The lawyer found the strangers lounging on their bunks, smoking cigarettes of Bull Durham and looking, in his opinion, less resentful than they should. He leaned against the bars of the celldoor and made his pitch.

"I'm a lawyer and it'd be my pleasure to represent you. I finally have Jason Teague and his old man right where I want them. You'll sue, naturally, and we'll take old Amos for a bundle. I'm not the only witness. The others won't be willing to testify, but they can be subpoenaed."

"You get the feellin' this jasper's totin' a heavy chip on his shoulder?" Stretch mildly enquired of his partner.

"The idea crossed my mind," said Larry.

"Who are you anyway?" asked Grade. "Damn it, the sheriff didn't even make a record of your names."

11

"I'm Lawrence, my partner's Wood-ville," drawled Larry. "And how come you're takin' that ruckus personal?"

"Come on." Grade grimaced impatiently. "Does anybody admire a cheat like Jason Teague, a show-off who feeds off his father's power and influence? Mayor Amos Teague's the biggest property owner in Porterville. Spencer, who runs the Red Rose, rents the premises from the old man. Hardly any local businessmen own their stores, their offices, the places where they conduct business, and they don't dare offend the Teagues. Young Jason's never taken a beating until today. The men he cheats and insults live in fear his father will raise their rent. That's power, and that's how power works."

"That your only reason for hatin' the dude's guts?" Larry quietly challenged.

Again, he read spite in Grade's bright eyes. Grade, he sensed, was full of it.

"Every eligible woman I've known, Jason Teague has lured them away from me," scowled the lawyer. "Gifts, flowers, suppers at the best restaurant in town."

"I guessed it had to be somethin' like that," said Larry. "Now why don't you take a walk."

"You *have* to sue!" pleaded Grade.

"No hurry," shrugged Larry.

"Hell, we only just got here," said Stretch. "Stabled our horses and ate lunch. I got a haircut and my compadre played a little poker. It's only been three-four hours." He thought to remark to Larry. "Didn't even get round to rentin' a room for the night."

"Now we won't have to," said Larry.

"Sure," grinned Stretch. "Three squares a day and a place to sleep — and the county pays."

"Now, listen . . . !" began Grade.

"You still here?" frowned Larry. "Vamoose, sorehead. If we decide we need you, we'll send for you."

An hour after the lawyer's angry departure, a grey-bearded man of slight physique was ushered into the cell-block by the sheriff, who introduced him to the prisoners as Amos Teague, Mayor of Porterville, and urged them show him proper respect. He unlocked the celldoor for the mayor, who moved across to perch on the end of Larry's bunk. The Texans noted the fine quality of his townsuit, the gold watchchain, the expensive high hat.

"Just call me when you're through, Mister Mayor," muttered Brentnall.

He returned to his office. Teague removed his hat, set it on his knees, surveyed the impassive Texans and began talking.

"Well, you know who I am and I suppose Frank Brentnall's advice fell on deaf ears. You've seen a sample of my son's behaviour, so how could I expect you to show me respect?"

"Spoilin' a son's the dumbest thing a father can do," chided Larry. "Don't you know what he is? In a poker party, he don't play square. He cheats and . . . "

"I know," sighed Teague. "And lies,

taking advantage of the family name, using our relationship to bully and bluff and get his own way. Spoiled rotten you'd say, and you'd be right. But — until there's some change — I have to placate his victims, pay his debts on the quiet, buy people off."

"You're hopin' *he'll* change?" challenged Larry. "It seems to me you're hopin' for too much."

"Not Jason," said Teague. "His mother, my beloved wife. A good woman, but foolish, too soft on the boy. It was she who spoiled him and, when I realized things were getting out of hand, I asserted my authority and began clamping down on his excesses." He bowed his head. "Unfortunately, Hattie was then stricken, became seriously ill. This is no ploy, gentlemen. You don't have to take my word. You're welcome to check with her physician, Doctor George Alvison."

"And sonny boy's the apple of her eye," guessed Stretch.

"She dotes on him," declared Teague.

15

"We keep her in ignorance of — the kind of person he's become, I, the doctor, our servants and friends. If she were to learn the truth about him, it could be tragic. Maybe she'll recover. George is doing everything medically possible. But — you now understand my predicament, I hope." The Texans were silent, trading thoughtful frowns. He eyed them pleadingly. "Jason deserves punishment, no question about that. I could argue he's suffering punishment right now, confined to a bed at the doctor's house. You really hurt him, if that's any satisfaction to you."

"You sayin' I was too rough on him?" muttered Larry.

"Well . . . " The mayor shrugged and winced. "Vern Beale, the bouncer at the Red Rose, is no lightweight. Jason has a broken arm, broken collarbone and two cracked ribs, and he'll probably lose a front tooth." He offered cigars. The tall men shook their heads. Lighting one for himself, he waxed business-like. "All right now, you've got me

16

over a barrel, so what's your price? For Hattie's sake, I don't want her to learn the true facts behind our son's injuries. I'm well aware Grade — that grudge-toting buzzard — has offered to represent you, urged you to sue. What will it cost me to have you leave town quietly? No problem about your release. I'll arrange that with the sheriff. Also I'll compensate Al Spencer for damages and — uh — the medical expenses of his staff. So how much? A hundred — two hundred . . . ?"

Again the Texans traded frowns. Then Stretch shrugged unconcernedly and Larry told Teague,

"We don't know yet."

"What does *that* mean?" demanded Teague.

"Means we only got to pay for board and feed of our horses and pick up a few supplies, few things we need," said Larry. "Twenty-five'll likely be too much. Closer to twenty I figure. We won't know till we're saddled up and ready to move out."

Teague blinked incredulously.

"That's all you'll ask of me — a few dollars?"

"We got no use for big dinero," drawled Larry, patting his hip pocket. "I calculate we're holdin' better'n five hundred right now."

"More'n enough for the likes of us," Stretch said casually, "We gamble a lot, toil when we have to, and just drift."

The mayor's cigar seemed to have lost its taste. He stared at its glowing tip and said softly.

"Gentlemen, you shame me. I feel I — should apologize for offering to buy you off."

"Don't worry about it," said Larry.

"Independent spirits," Teague realized. "Proud. Too much so to take advantage of my situation."

"Chances are you're the richest hombre in this territory," said Larry. "But I wouldn't trade places with you for every buck you got. We can take care of our kind of trouble. I don't know how you'll ever take care of yours."

"I have to get home, check on my wife," said Teague, rising, producing a well-filled wallet. "Mightn't be anywhere near Main Street when you're ready to leave. How about fifty to help you on your way?"

"Twenty," the Texans said firmly.

The Mayor of Porterville placed two $10 bills on the bunk, retreated to the celldoor and called to Brentnall. They were talking quietly as they returned to the sheriff's office, leaving the trouble-prone nomads to ponder the problems of wealthy men with ailing wives and selfish, wayward sons.

Significantly, the Texans were very much at ease in this cell. It had all happened before, disputes, brawls in trail-town saloons, stores, livery stables or main streets. Violence seemed to dog them everywhere they roamed, and they had roamed far since quitting their homestate long years before, victims of their wanderlust. Town rowdies, saloon bouncers, cardsharps and such were not of course their most dangerous adversaries. They had and would continue to lock horns with more homicidal assailants, the rustler gangs, the hold-up artists hitting banks and stage-lines. Larry Valentine and Stretch Emerson had not set out to become trouble-shooters, outlaw-fighters of formidable reputation, circulation boosters for frontier newspapers, a thorn in the sides of countless lawmen resenting their record of desperadoes front and defeated. They were just as unpopular with certain big shots of the Pinkerton Detective Agency and the Department of Justice and the U.S. Army. But not by intent. To this day, they still claimed to be peace-loving, a couple of footloose drifters bent only on minding their own business and riding clear of strife and upheaval; thanks to the machinations of fickle Fate, it hadn't worked out that way.

"Where to from here?" asked Stretch, the tone of his question suggesting the answer was of little importance.

"Well, we ain't exactly a million miles from the Nevada border, are we?" drawled Larry. "So I'm for quittin' California."

"Suits me," shrugged Stretch.

A few minutes later, the sheriff released them as per the mayor's instructions. They strapped on their sidearms, won a scowl from Brentnall by warning him against playing poker with Teague's son and sauntered out to find a general store. Sundown was still ninety minutes in the future when the tall men left Porterville behind them and pointed the sorrel and pinto eastward, their destination the state of Nevada.

★ ★ ★

In the spacious drawing room of a mansion in Sacramento, the will of the late Ellie Marchmount, widow of one of California's best known mining tycoons, was being read to beneficiaries at about the same time two tough Texans were beating the living daylights out of five adversaries in a Porterville saloon.

Presiding was Warren Abel, elderly but durable, the family lawyer since time immemorial. The two couples sharing a magnificent Chesterfield were the Marchmount sons, Bandford and Samuel, and their spouses, Lucille and Dora. Since the demise of their sire, the sons had jointly administered the high-profit Marchmount Mineral Enterprises. California born and raised, they were business leaders of distinction and looked the part. Custom tailored, they were as impressive as their fashionably-gowned wives.

Filling an easy chair, a nephew, only son of the late Cluther Marchmount's only sister, stroked his mustache and puffed on a cigar. He wasn't the kind to request permission to smoke, this Clive Renfield, a bulky man whose increasing girth testified to his fondness of rich food and the high life. With his mane of dark hair, he might have been considered handsome. The defects were a blotchy complexion and a double chin.

Seated side by side and looking out of place in such luxurious surroundings were the Dobsons of Northeast Nevada, Kitty, the youngest woman present, and her husband. Pete Dobson was a cattleman, a small rancher, his compact body packed into a store-bought suit, his celluloid collar giving him hell. To please his wife, he wore the suit, celluloid collar and black string necktie, but had refused to purchase a derby; his Stetson perched on his lap. He was sun-browned and even-featured, his wife dark-haired and passably attractive; he considered her beautiful and could not be overawed by the fashionable attire and airs and graces of Lucille and Dora.

Kitty was self-conscious of her travelling gown and a bonnet that had seen better days, but clinging tenaciously to her dignity, trying not to notice the amused appraisal of the other women.

"I, Eleanor Denby Marchmount, being of sound mind and body . . . " began Abel.

"Get to the handouts, Abel," urged Renfield. "Who ends up with what? We don't need the preamble."

The brothers and their wives eyed him askance. For obvious reasons, he was regarded as no gentleman. His manners left plenty to be desired and it was well-known he was a wastrel, preferring to spend his time in the state capital's lower class district, patronizing gambling palaces and houses of ill repute. Bradford and Samuel Marchmount were also aware that his frequent visits to their mother were prompted by greed and shortage of cash rather than sociability.

Lucille and Dora shrugged disdainfully. The Dobsons sat quiet, not knowing how to react to the interruption. The lawyer nodded coolly.

"As you wish, Mister Renfield," he

said. "I'll proceed to the bequests as listed in the will."

First on the list of beneficiaries were the servants who had tended the old lady during her last years and long illness. Renfield interjected during Abel's announcement of the bequests, remarking it was typical of his late aunt that she should think first of the hired help. The lawyer let that pass and carried on.

The old family mansion, all other real estate, cash in the Marchmount bank account, stocks, bonds and ownership of Marchmount Mineral Enterprises were to be shared by the brothers.

"That's pretty much what we expected," nodded the elder brother.

"And quite fair," commented Samuel.

"Oh, sure, why wouldn't you be crowing?" growled Renfield. "The hog's share."

"Which will be in efficient hands," Dora said aloofly.

"Brad, dear, I don't believe we need postpone our European tour any longer," said Lucille.

"Making plans already," grouched Renfield. "Come on, Abel, there's more, isn't there? Get on with it."

"To my nephew, Clive Renfield," quoted the lawyer. "The entire wardrobe of my late beloved husband, Cluther Marchmount."

"That's it?" challenged Renfield, reddening. "That's all I get?"

"An extensive wardrobe, let me assure you, sir," said Abel. "Evening attire, suits of the finest quality, shirts . . . "

"None of it'll fit me," protested Renfield. "The old jasper's hand-me-down clothes? What do I need with . . . ?"

"That is for you to decide," said Abel. "You'll find your inheritance in two trunks and the closet and dresser of the guestroom at the end of the first floor corridor. May I go on? There is a final bequest."

"By all means, Mister Abel," drawled Lucille. "Time does seem to be dragging, and I have an appointment with my milliner later this afternoon."

"To my niece, Katharine Ames Dobson, only child of my beloved baby sister Margaret . . . " intoned Abel. He paused, winced uncomfortably and kept his eyes on the document, "who after her marriage and re-location far from this city, did not forget me, but corresponded regularly, her letters a joy and comfort to me in my declining years." He paused again, directing his gaze at Kitty. "Not her own words, Mrs Dobson. She asked me express her affection for you in formal terms."

"I understand," nodded Kitty.

"Well, are we to be kept in suspense?" challenged Dora.

"I'm just dying to hear," smiled Lucille.

"Well — ahem — its what some might consider an unusual bequest," said Abel. "An item of female underwear, Mrs Dobson. To be precise . . . " He averted his eyes, "a corset."

27

Kitty's eyebrows shot up. Her husband dropped his gaze to the dented crown of his Stetson. Renfield guffawed and slapped his knee. The brothers traded grins. Dora giggled.

"Is that everything?" demanded Lucille.

"That concludes the reading of the will," nodded Abel. "Mrs Dobson, your — uh — inheritance is in a wrapped box on your late aunt's bed."

"One of the dear old soul's cast-offs, I presume?" murmured Lucille, while Kitty flushed in embarrassment.

"I believe not, Mrs Marchmount," Abel said primly. "I think Mrs Dobson will find the — item — is new."

"Hold everything, Abel." Renfield was no longer amused. "Something important's been overlooked. Who gets the Sierra Stash?"

"Oh, that old rumor?" shrugged Lucille.

"No rumor, my dear, unless Dad lied about it from the time Sam and I were just boys," frowned Bradford. "And I honestly don't believe he'd lie about it, just invent a legend."

"Let people say what they will," muttered his brother. "Our father was never an eccentric. Only a keen mind could found Marchmount Enterprises and build it to a multi-million dollar concern."

"He used to call it that," Bradford remarked to the lawyer. "His Sierra Stash, his nest egg of gold nuggets to the value of — what would be your estimate, Sam?"

"On today's gold prices, the current market, I'd say a hundred thousand at least, possibly more," said his brother.

"He made a map of the spot where he hid it — *must* have," insisted Renfield. "Would he risk not being able to find it again if he ever needed it? Why, he staked a claim and mined that fortune far back when he was a young prospector."

"Logical that he'd draw a map," Samuel conceded. "On the other hand, none of us ever saw it. It's possible our mother did, though I wouldn't swear to that either."

"There has to be a map!" asserted Renfield. "So why wasn't that cache of gold included in his will — or the old girl's?"

"I can only conclude it *is* a myth, Mister Renfield," said Abel. "Believe me, Mrs Marchmount never mentioned it when I was summoned to draw up this document. You'll all receive copies, naturally. Peruse *this* copy if you wish." He proffered the document to Renfield, who scowled and shook his head. "A jest, perhaps."

"A family joke," opined Dora. "Now, Brad, both your parents tended to be a little whimsical."

"Their sense of humor," remarked Lucille. "Quite droll at times."

"He did stash a big part of his first gold strike," declared Renfield. "He didn't use all of it to set himself up in business, so the rest of it's still in the mountains, still where he cached it — and there *must* be a *map*!" Impulsively, he quit his chair. "His clothes! That could be it! Secret pocket of an old coat maybe, or hidden in the lining!"

"The guestroom, Mister Renfield," the lawyer repeated, as Renfield dashed from the room.

"Well, I think you've covered everything, Mister Abel," said the elder brother, and the Marchmounts rose to leave. Though of humble origin, Pete Dobson would not be found wanting where the essential courtesies were concerned. He got to his feet and nodded respectfully to his wife's cousins. "Nice seeing you again, Pete. Ranch coming along well I take it?"

"Plenty to be done," muttered Pete. "But it'll get done. Takes time, you know?"

"Well, actually, I don't know," grinned Bradford. "The cattle business is out of my line. Remember the name of the family business — Marchmount *Mineral* Enterprises?"

"Yeah, sure," nodded Pete.

The Marchmounts departed. Abel accorded Kitty a bow, shook hands with Pete and took his leave. A room-maid then conducted the younger couple upstairs. Kitty, linking arms with her husband, said softly,

"I'm so terribly *sorry* . . . "

"You don't have to be," he assured her. "Just don't fret about it, honey. If you want to talk, wait till we get back to the hotel."

In the master bedroom, the maid discreetly withdrew. Kitty moved to the bed, picked up the parcel and held it to her breast.

"I'm grateful to her anyway," she murmured. "We *were* close, Pete, and I enjoyed her letters as much as she enjoyed mine and — I won't forget her."

"And you oughtn't," he nodded. "Well, you ready to go?"

She nodded, took his arm again and, still clutching the parcel, moved with him into the corridor. Over the sounds he was making, opening trunks, pulling out dresser drawers, tearing garments once worn by the famous Cluther Marchmount, Renfield must have heard them close the door. He emerged from the guestroom and came toward them and his suggestive leer caused Pete Dobson's eyes to narrow.

33

# 2

## Two Schemers And a Snooper

"LEAVING already?" asked Renfield. "Not me. I'll find that map if I have to check every inch of everything the old jasper ever wore." He eyed them insolently. "What's your hurry?"

"We have to get back to our hotel," said Kitty. "A little packing before supper."

"Got quite a ways to travel," her husband pointed out.

"So we need to take the morning train east-bound out of Sacramento," explained Kitty. "It'll put us in Bellamy, Nevada. From there we have to travel all the way home by stagecoach."

"Oh, sure," nodded Renfield. "All the way home to — what's it called, that hick burg you come from? Scuttle Bucket Creek?"

"Scudder Creek," said Pete. "Our spread's a little ways southeast of the township."

"I took it for granted you'd want to try on your inheritance for size, cousin, what with the old girl's bedroom available," grinned Renfield. "Might be the most fun your man's had since you got here."

Kitty flushed angrily.

"Clive Renfield, you're no gentleman!"

"Listen, Renfield, I don't much appreciate the way your mouth works," growled Pete. "That's no way to talk to my wife — and it better be the last time, savvy?"

"What're you gonna do, cowboy, pull a six-shooter on me?" Renfield flinched, feigning alarm and mimicking Pete's mode of speech. "Shucks, pardner, I didn't mean nothin'. No call for you to git riled."

"I got a mind to . . . " began Pete, bunching his fists.

"Let's just leave, Pete," begged Kitty. "Please?"

Her husband aimed a scowl at Renfield. She took his arm and they made for the stairs, while Renfield hurried back to the guest room to resume his search.

Pete donned his Stetson after they were clear of the mansion and beginning a long walk to the less salubrious area of the big city. He had wanted to rent a rig for transporting them to the upper crust district and back to their humble hotel, but Kitty had refused to permit this. Their travelling money had to be conserved. They had their return train tickets and cash enough for stage passage from Bellamy to their hometown and very little more. P-Bar-D was just getting started, a small ranch with a small herd, and not yet a paying proposition.

"It's a big disappointment," she sighed. "I don't mean to sound greedy, but I was hoping . . . "

"Enjoy the scenery and quit your

fretting," he soothed. "Chances are we'll never see Sacramento again, Kitty honey."

"I still love Aunt Ellie and always will," she declared. "But, if she'd left me *some* money, even just a few hundred dollars, we could put it to such good use. When I got the lawyer's letter . . . "

"Inviting your presence, it said, as I recall," he mused. "For the reading of the will of the late . . . "

"I was so sure, Pete," she complained.

"We'll get by," he said firmly. "I didn't marry you because you had rich kinfolk."

"My parents were so poor when they died," she said sadly. "Dad was never as shrewd with money as Uncle Clute. Everything he invested in just — came to nothing."

"Listen, there'll always be rich folks and poor folks," he shrugged. "And there'll always be in-betweens like us, never getting rich, but thankful for a roof over our heads, enough food and

37

the chance the spread'll grow."

Later, in their room at the cheapest hotel they could find, Kitty reprimanded herself.

"I must've sounded greedy and I'm sorry I talked that way."

"Now you're making sense," he approved, hanging his coat and hat, flopping into a chair. "And I'll tell you something, Mrs Peter Durand Dobson. I wouldn't trade my wife for those high-falutin' females your cousins're wed to, them with their fancy gowns and their snoots in the air, no siree."

"When their noses weren't in the air, they were looking down them at us," she recalled. "I suppose, to them, we seem like . . . "

"Never you mind how we seem to Lucille and Dora," he chided, fishing out Durham sack and cigarette papers. "Why don't you try on Aunt Ellie's gift?"

"Why not," she nodded, unfastening her gown.

A thought occurred to him after he'd

rolled and lit his cigarette.

"I don't savvy somethin'. How'd she know if you could use it? Two years we've been man and wife and I never got curious about such a thing before. Do they have to be made special, or . . . ?"

"Men," she said in exasperation. "You're right about one thing, Pete Dobson. There's a lot the married ones *never* learn about ladies' underwear. Corsets come in sizes, and she knew my size."

"She did?" he grinned.

"I must've mentioned it in a letter some time ago." She had removed gown and petticoats. Now, as she began unfastening her corset, an item much the worse for wear, her face clouded over. "Back when — we thought we . . ."

His grin faded as he gruffly reminded her,

"We made a deal. We wouldn't look back — and get sad about it any more."

"It grieves a woman, Pete" she told him. "A miscarriage is an unhappy memory."

"Keep thinking of what Doc Seeley said," he advised. "No bad damage. We'll have kids. It'll happen in the Lord's good time."

She unwrapped the parcel. The paper had covered a flat box, the lid of which she now raised to inspect the new undergarment. Her expression was wistful as she held it up.

"Pink," he noted, working up another grin. "Mighty pretty. Too bad nobody else'll ever see it."

"So beautifully made," she murmured. "Dear old Aunt Ellie. We were so fond of each other. I shouldn't say it, but my cousins . . . " She shook her head sadly.

"I guess they were loyal to her, loved her in their own way, and she was proud of them, only . . . "

"Only they're big shots now, Brad and Sam, and a couple of stuffed shirts," he said.

"As for Clive . . . " she began.

"Hey, he's bad medicine," frowned Pete. "Best we forget about him."

"That'll be a pleasure," she assured him, as she began fitting herself into the corset.

★ ★ ★

Around 7 o'clock that evening, two of Sacramento's minor lawbreakers pursued their regular routine. They were petty thieves of no account, Jed and Elmer, scathingly referred to by major crime figures as a couple of penny ante scavengers and almost ignored by the state capital's law authorities. As well as being small-time, Jed Kinch and Elmer Biddle tended to be more than a little inept; if they made a score, it was usually a lucky accident. Jed, the skinny one, was the snooper of the partnership, spending most of his time eavesdropping, picking up pieces of information of potential value. Tubby Elmer's specialty was pocket-picking.

41

While Elmer tried his luck and skill on pedestrians in the Montgomery Square and Battery Street regions, Jed prowled the area east of the Armijo district, moving in and out of cheap dives, keeping a sharp eye out for open or half-open windows of rooms whose occupants might unwittingly put him onto a good thing.

As it happened, Clive Renfield had visited one of his own kind after his abortive search of the Cluther Marchmount wardrobe. Herb Berman, an ex-member of the infamous Hamill gang of Nevada outlaws, plied the cardsharp's trade nowadays and had become Renfield's close crony. In Berman's quarters, a ground-floor rear room of a cheap lodging house, they discussed the news circulated by Sacramento's evening papers, the revelation that the will of Cluther Marchmount's widow had been read minus reference to the famous Sierra Stash.

As it also happened, Jed Kinch read

such newspapers as had been consigned to trash bins and was in the immediate vicinity at this time. His venal curiosity having been aroused, he was hunkered under a half-open window, keenly interested in what Renfield and his crony had to say.

"The Marchmount brothers are the big winners," Renfield complained, as Berman refilled his glass. "They inherit the whole business. Well, that was no surprise, but why no mention of the old man's cache in the Sierras?"

"I never believed it was a rumor," drawled Berman, a lean individual with sharp features crowned by a pomaded thatch. "There's been talk of it for better than twenty years. It's there all right, wherever old Clute buried it, a fortune in pure nuggets. Some hiding place he must've found, huh? I mean, for it to stay hidden so long. And I agree — there has to be a map."

"I'm never gonna uncover the stash," scowled Renfield, "until I've found that damn map."

"So all the old lady left you was Clute's clothes," mused Berman. "Anybody else get lucky?"

"No luckier than me," said Renfield. "Cousin Kitty Dobson, the old girl's favorite relative, was counting on a fat bundle of cash, she and her husband." He grinned mirthlessly. "If you could've seen her face when the lawyer read it out, told her all she inherited was a corset. How do you like *that* for a laugh? A corset!"

"Quite a joker, Ellie Marchmount," commented Berman.

"Can you imagine, Herb?" chuckled Renfield. "All the way from some hick place far northeast in Nevada the Dobsons came, hoping to pick up a handy parcel of money. Now they have to travel all the way home — with nothing but that damn corset."

Berman sipped bourbon and frowned thoughtfully.

"When do they leave?" he asked.

"They'll be on the early eastbound tomorrow," shrugged Renfield. "They

44

quit the train at Bellamy, Nevada. That's a junction town. From there, they'll have to switch to a Wells Fargo coach headed northeast."

"This Dobson woman," prodded Berman. "The old lady's favorite you say?"

"Used to write to each other," nodded Renfield. "Old Ellie had a real soft spot for her youngest relative I can tell you. I couldn't be so fortunate. Visited the old girl all the time, did my damnedest to sweeten her up, but could I ever get a dime out of her? Not so you'd notice."

Berman's interest was increasing, and that went double for the unsuspected eavesdropper; by now, snooping Jed was trembling with excitement.

"Friend, we're onto something, but it hasn't hit you yet," muttered Berman.

"I've missed something?" challenged Renfield.

"Think a minute," urged Berman. "We're agreed old Clute must've mapped the location of his cache.

It's logical he told his wife about it. After he cashed in his chips, it was hers, but she was well provided for, her sons too, so she had no need of it. Knowing she'd soon be as dead as her husband, what do you suppose she'd do with it? Wouldn't just burn it, would she? No sense to that. A fortune in gold that nobody can ever find? No, she had to pass it on — and who would she most likely leave it to? Her favorite'd be my guess. Doesn't that figure? And didn't you say the Dobson woman's husband's a near broke rancher?"

"It's as if you haven't been listening," chided Renfield. "I told you all Kitty Dobson inherited was a damn-blasted corset."

"Sure, you told me," nodded Berman. "So, if you had to make a guess, where would you guess the old lady hid the map to the Marchmount cache?"

Renfield's eyes popped. He swore explosively.

"I should've realized!" he gasped. "If she thought so highly of her loving niece, she wouldn't just leave her . . . !"

"Not just a piece of underwear, Clive," opined Berman. "Something special. The map. Easy enough to hide it that way."

"It's sewed into the — hey!" breathed Renfield. "She's probably wearing the damn thing right now!"

"And, sooner or later, she's gonna find it," warned Berman. Then, glancing to his right, he decided, "We're getting into something big now. I'd better close the window."

In the time it took Berman to rise, set his glass down and move across to the window, the snooper had pulled a fast disappearing trick. Jed Kinch was out of that back alley when the window was pulled down and locked. He figured he had heard more than enough, and all of it potentially profitable to a couple of deserving cases, namely Messrs J. Kinch and E. Biddle.

Returning to his chair, Berman eyed Renfield challengingly. Renfield promptly insisted,

47

"We got more use for that fortune than Cousin Kitty and her cowpoke husband. I want that map."

"We'll get it," promised Berman. "But this is a special situation, kind of delicate. With Reno Hamill and my old buddies, I've taken hard cash from bank safes, ran off cattle and hit many a stagecoach. At planning any kind of hold up, Reno's the best, a real expert, and that's why he's still on the loose."

"We won't need . . . " began Renfield.

"We *could* need Reno and what's left of the old outfit," predicted Berman. "All right, that'd mean equal shares all round when we dig up the cache, but we should fret? Hell, Clive, we're talking about a fortune in raw gold. Divvy it eight, nine, a dozen ways, and every man still ends up with a bundle."

"You could find Hamill's bunch — if we need help" frowned Renfield.

"They hole up in a hideaway no

posse has ever gotten within three miles of," said Berman. "I could find it again — easily. It's southeast of Bellamy in Nevada, where the Dobson will overnight day after tomorrow. The thing is, we could make Bellamy same time as the Dobsons."

"What do you mean — special situation — delicate?" demanded Renfield.

Berman grinned crookedly.

"You ever steal a corset before?" he asked. "I certainly haven't. It'll have to be well planned and the timing has to be right. Hell, Clive, you don't clobber a woman in Sacramento, Bellamy or any other town and just haul her into an alley, strip her and make off with her underwear."

"All right, I'm not dumb, you don't have to spell it out," muttered Renfield. "It'll have to be after they turn in. I don't reckon any female sleeps in her corset. But *we* try first, Herb. If we don't score at the hotel in Bellamy, that'll be time enough for you to call in your old friends."

"And they have a long haul ahead of'em after they roll out of Bellamy," Berman pointed out. "From there to Scudder Creek, there'll be a hundred and one ambush sites Hamill knows of." He checked his watch again. "Two things we have to do now. Buy passage on the train to Bellamy, then a change of clothes. Something rough I'd say. Work clothes. We'll need to look a whole lot different in Bellamy, can't take a chance the Dobsons'll sight you and recognize you."

They drained their glasses, donned their hats and made for the railroad terminal while, four blocks away, Jed Kinch finally sighted his sidekick. Pudgy Elmer Biddle was furtively entering a side alley. Jed followed him and, upon reaching him, seized him by an arm.

"Pssstt! It's me!"

"Don't *do* that!" gasped Elmer. "Jumpin' Julius, you scared hell outa me!"

"You been gettin' lucky?" demanded Jed.

"Couple wallets," Elmer reported.

"You can check 'em in the hayloft, the barn where our horses're at," said Jed, hustling him to the rear of the alley. "We're ridin', pal, just as soon as we buy us some supplies. It's Nevada for us! We're gonna get rich!"

"What the hell're you talkin' about?"

"Tell you when we can parley private."

In the hayloft a short time later, Elmer checked the contents of two purloined wallets by moon-light shafting in through a crack.

"Did better tonight," he calculated. "Near ninety bucks."

"Good enough for starters," leered Jed. "But small potaters, Elmer ol' pal. Me and you, we're gonna find the Sierra Stash!"

"All that cached Marchmount gold, old Clute's first find?" grinned Elmer. "Hot damn!"

"We'll find the stash on accounta

51

there's a map and I know who's got it, only she dunno she's got it," chuckled Jed.

"Tell me that again," begged Elmer. "Slow, so I can savvy it."

The gist of an overheard conversation was repeated for Elmer's enlightenment, after which Jed bragged this project was what every felon dreams of when now he lays him down to sleep.

"Glory hallelujah," breathed Elmer. "I been hearin' 'bout the Sierra Stash since back when my voice broke. And it was in all the papers tonight. Old Clute's widder up and died and — wait a minute — there was nothin' in the will 'bout no map to no stash."

"I told you," grinned Jed. "Them dudes I spied on figured it out. Only one place it could be hid."

"I'm gettin' nervous," winced Elmer. "How do we steal one of them contraptions off of the female that's usin' it to pull herself together? Ain't like stealin' a bonnet, Jed. You can grab a hat and skedaddle and that's that. Them corset things now, they're tricky. I never unhitched no female out of her stays, but I don't reckon as how it'd be easy. We couldn't do it fast — and she'd be screamin' blue murder."

"I've been studyin' on that," said Jed. "Got it whittled down to the two times a woman ain't wearin' such a thing."

"What two times?" asked Elmer.

"What d'you mean — *what* two times?" Jed impatiently challenged. "When they're takin' a bath and when they call it a day, hit the old feathers, hush-a-bye. They don't sleep in them things."

"I'm still leery on accounta I dunno much about women," fretted Elmer. "Hell, I dunno *nothin'* about women."

"It's sure fire," Jed assured him. "We get us some grub for the trail, take a look-see at a chart at the railroad depot or the Wells Fargo office, plan us a straight route to Bellamy and get there round about the time the train rolls in. Then we bust into their room real late and one of us keeps her man covered while one of us grabs the thing-ummyjig. Then we vamoose somewheres quiet where we can cut it up and find the map. Then we head for the Sierra Nevada and dig up the cache. We won't have to search all over the dratted high country, Elmer. We'll have the map, and it'll lead us right to the stash!" He gestured urgently. "C'mon, let's get down outa here and saddle up and sneak out while the hostler's wettin' his whistle at the bar across the street."

That was how the treasure hunt began, two shabby small-time thieves in dented derby hats riding for the Nevada border forty-five minutes later, Renfield and Berman buying range clothes and planning on making the early morning departure on the train carrying the Dobsons. First an item of female underwear would be acquired after which, having vandalized said item, the lucky thieves would possess a map that would lead them to the famous Sierra Stash. To all greed-crazed parties concerned, it all seemed easy. But, as all gamblers are well aware, Lady Luck is a fickle jade and fortunes aren't always made as a result of best laid plans.

The eastbound train was scheduled to overnight at Virginia City, which was growing fast and, in the opinion of Herb Berman, not a safe place for breaking into a hotel room.

"Too much law," he warned Renfield next morning. They were boarding the second Pullman car after noting the Dobsons were in the car ahead. "Give it another year, and Virgina City'll have as big a population as Carson. Last time I was there, city police patrolled all night."

"Yeah, so better we make our move in Bellamy," agreed Renfield. "Well, I pointed her out, so you'll know her when the time comes."

When they were seated, Berman remarked,

"Her man, the rancher jasper, wasn't packing a pistol."

"My guess is he brought it along, one of those big Colts," muttered Renfield. "But he's a rube who wouldn't call it polite to show a sidearm in a big city."

The eastbound departed on schedule and, gazing out a window, Berman began speculating.

"When word spreads, the old lady gone, the will read, a lot of optimists'll head for the Sierras. It's happened a dozen times since Clute Marchmount founded his business and bragged of his first strike."

"Newspapers'll make sure the whole damn country knows," opined Renfield.

"Lucky old sonofabitch," grimaced Berman. "He could afford to stash most of it. What he brought into Sacramento years ago was more than enough to set himself up. He bought mines that were supposed to be played out, did a lot of investing and, from then on, couldn't make a wrong move.

He had the Midas touch, that's a fact."

"Cousin Sam estimates the cache'd be worth a hundred thousand," said Renfield, licking his lips.

Berman dropped his voice before confiding,

"I've killed for as little as a hundred bucks — so heaven help your cousin's cowboy husband if he gets in my way."

"If you have to settle Dobson's hash, it'd better be done quietly," cautioned Renfield.

"I'm as fast with a knife as with a Smith and Wesson," Berman assured him. "Don't worry. He'll get his, but quietly."

★ ★ ★

Two p.m. of the day the eastbound would reach Bellamy, the Texans were headed in the general direction of Nevada's Shoshone Mountains, craving solitude and hoping to get in some hunting. They were to postpone the hunting trip, thanks to their chance meeting with Billy Morke, chuck-boss of a Bellamy County spread, the Quarter Circle.

They were crossing the trail some thirty-five yards ahead of the north-bound rig when its driver waved to them. Urgently they thought, so they reined up and waited. Old Billy brought his team to a halt, growling at the animals with the mouthpiece of an old brier pipe clamped between his teeth.

"Plumb thankful I run into *somebody*." He gave his name and begged a light. "Nary a match in my doggone pockets. Plenty in back with the supplies, but I'd have to shift a couple sacks of flour to get at' em."

"Sure," shrugged Larry.

He gave the chuck-boss a match and leaned from his saddle to tuck some spares into a pocket of the tattered vest. Billy Morke seemed in a talkative mood. They were in no hurry, so hooked legs about their saddlehorns and fished out their makings. While they rolled cigarettes, Morke got his pipe working, puffed a blue cloud and complained, "He's still holdin' out on me."

"That so?" prodded Larry, grinning indulgently.

Stretch obliged by showing curiosity. The trouble-shooters liked old people, male or female and no matter how garrulous.

"Who's he?" he asked.

"Stendahl — consarn him," grouched Morke. "I beg. I near to get on my knees, but durned if he'll tell me."

"That's a damn shame," Larry sympathized.

"Chris Stendahl," offered Morke. "You never heard of him?" The Texans shook their heads apologetically. "Must be new in this territory. Yup. I don't recollect seein' you bucks before. What do I call you?"

"He's Lawrence, I'm Woodville," said Stretch.

"Pleased to meetcha," Morke acknowledged. He puffed on his old brier and peered into the distance at nothing in particular, but resentfully. "So it's still his secret, and he ain't lettin' on to nobody."

"Stendahl," guessed Larry.

"Yup," nodded Morke. "By golly, I'll tell you, if I knew how he does it, I could do it too. I'd have the bunkhouse gang at the old Quarter Circle droolin'. I could put the arm on Buck Halliday — he's the boss — put the arm on him for double what he pays me. And he'd have to pay it because, if I threatened to quit, every hand on his payroll'd back me."

"I just bet they would," agreed Stretch.

The chuck-boss brooded. The drifters traded covert grins, lit their cigarettes and waited patiently.

"So," shrugged Morke. "If you're strangers in these here parts, I guess you never heard of Stendahl's steaks."

"No," said Larry. "We never did."

"All kindsa eateries in the county seat," remarked Morke. "Two Chinese places. Even the Gay Paree on Piper Street where it's all French cookin'. But Stendahl's Steakhouse is where a man goes if he hankers for beef the likes of which he never ate before. I'm tellin' you the way him and his wife do a T-bone, for instance, it's like a durn miracle. By golly. Tender as a young girl's kiss. And the taste! Man alive, what I wouldn't give to know how he does it. But I couldn't be so lucky. It'll always be his secret."

"*That* good?" challenged Larry.

"Boy, you never had a steak like they dish up at the Stendahl place," sighed Morke. "Melt in your mouth. Meat fit for a king."

Stretch's mouth watered. The Texans had cooked and eaten a fulsome lunch around twenty after high noon, but he suddenly had an appetite again.

"Uh, runt . . . " he began pleadingly.

"You don't have to say it," muttered Larry. "I got the same feelin'. And wouldn't Billy know? He's a ranch cook. So, if he says . . . "

"I'm tellin' you true," declared Morke. "If you never cut into a Stendahl steak, you dunno what you're missin'." He jerked a thumb. "And you're lucky. Just foller this trail south nice and steady and you'll make the county seat come sundown." He heaved a sigh. "If I could fix steaks so good, I'd be the proudest feller in this whole state. Well, best be movin' along."

"Be seein' you, Billy," nodded Larry, as the wagon rolled past. He then remarked to his partner, "When we quit Porterville, we vowed we'd stay clear of towns for as long as our supplies hold out. We're still totin' plenty of everything, but . . . "

"I just changed my mind," Stretch said eagerly.

"I just changed mine too," said Larry. "Don't care a damn if the badge-toters of this territory are ornery as hell and Texas-haters from way back, don't care if we get prodded into a dozen fights, just so long as we get to eat Stendahl's steaks."

"You notice the look on old Billy's face? He's so jealous of Stendahl's cookin', it was breakin' his heart."

"I noticed. So what're we waitin' for?"

"We ain't waitin', runt. We ain't waitin'."

And that was the only reason the case-hardened drifters headed south for Bellamy. A valid and logical reason. Legal too. Seeking only to sample the Stendahl cuisine, did they deserve the strife, the tension, the danger in store for them? But that was the way of it; their hex still clung to them like a wet slicker.

At 4.15 and from a distance, Bellamy looked orderly and well settled. They resolved to stable their mounts, check into a hotel and patronize a saloon for the purpose of downing an appetizer or two before presenting themselves at Stendahl's Steakhouse.

Entering the main street as unobtrusively as they were able, they followed it downtown to the railroad station, passing the Wells Fargo depot en route. The Givney Hotel was located almost directly opposite the railroad station and a livery stable, Colyer's, only a short distance north of it. They left Larry's sorrel and Stretch's pinto there and hefted their gear along to the hotel, where the desk clerk informed them their luck was in. A vacancy for them, a second-floor double.

"Eastbound train gets in soon," he explained. "We'd be full up if a couple of drummers hadn't checked out this morning. Have to reserve accommodation for folks staying overnight, you know?"

"That's as long as we'll stay I think," said Larry, proffering money.

The tall strangers signed the register, were given a key and climbed to Room 4 to stash their packrolls, saddlebags and sheathed Winchesters. They then quit the hotel and made for the nearest saloon, its shingle and emblem identifying it as the Four Leaf Clover.

Breasting the bar, hooking boot-heels on the brass rail, they ordered beer and, while slaking their thirst, listened to quite a dissertation from the gabby barkeep.

Bellamy County, he proudly advised them, was crime-free territory except for a once in a while minor disturbance, thanks to the local council's having secured the services of the three Chugg brothers as keepers of the peace.

"If you've heard of them Earps in Arizona, you've heard of the Chuggs?" he insisted.

Larry gave him an honest answer.

"We've heard of the Earps. We ain't heard of the Chuggs."

"Dick's our sheriff," bragged the barkeep. "His brothers Nick and Rick are his deputies and, believe me, they keep this county free of rustlers, cardsharps and stage robbers, every kind of badman you could name, keep all the rowdy cowhands in line too."

The strangers expressed gratitude that the peace of this community was in the hands of such reliable law officers, pointing out they themselves were men of peace. As well as being gabby, the barkeep was inquisitive.

"What brings you to Bellamy?" he wanted to know.

Larry decided another honest answer was called for, having noted in the bar mirror a heavyset, bushy-browed star-toter wearing two pistols and hovering close to listen.

# 3

## Don't Leave Town

STRETCH too had noted the reflection of a hulking Chugg, the beady eyes suspicious under the bushy brows. He showed the barkeep an amiable grin and declared,

"We're overnightin' here."

"Ran into the Quarter Circle chuck-boss along the trail," explained Larry.

"Old Billy, huh?" prodded the barkeep.

"Old Billy," nodded Larry. "And he bent our ears about a cafe in Bellamy that serves the greatest steaks anywhere."

"Oh, sure," said the barkeep. "Stendahl's. Billy steered you right, boys. A man eats hearty when he eats at Stendahl's."

"We can hardly wait," said Stretch.

The lawman shoved himself closer to them and growled a challenge and, for once, they found it easy to tight-rein their tempers. In truth, they were more amused than indignant. This badge-toter's aggressiveness was over-played. Comically so in their opinion.

"That all you're here for?" he demanded. "And you better answer up smart on account of maybe I've recognized you."

Larry surveyed him amiably while replying,

"Good steak supper, eight hours of peaceful sleep at the Givney Hotel and we're on our way right after breakfast."

"That better be true," the deputy warned. "Because us Chuggs never sleep at the same time. One of us is always wide awake and ready, savvy?"

"We're sure glad to hear that," said Stretch. "'Scuse me.

Which Jug're you? Mick, Vic or Chick?"

"The name's *Chugg!*" The hefty one glowered at him. "I'm young

68

Nick, Sheriff Dick's second deputy, and there's some say I'm meaner'n *Old* Nick. Now I'm gonna go check our records. Got me a notion I've seen your faces before. So don't leave town, hear?"

"Yes *sir*, Deputy," said Stretch.

Deputy Nick hurried out. Poker-faced, Larry remarked to the barkeep, "Some tough star-toter."

"The toughest, him and his brothers," asserted the barkeep. "It don't pay to tangle with 'em."

"We'll be real careful," promised Stretch.

They ordered refills while, at the law office, Deputy Nick tripped in his haste to clear the threshold and advanced purposefully to the file cabinet to check files. To his chagrin, the folder stuffed with circulars, subjects L. Valentine and W. E. Emerson, contained no warrants.

The Texans lingered at the Four Leaf Clover till the barkeep informed them Stendahl's would be open for business now. They heard the east-bound train approaching as they quit the saloon to seek the cafe, and only then did Stretch give vent to his mirth.

"If we've heard of the Earps . . . " he chuckled, "we ought've heard of the Chuggs!"

"All of Deputy Nick's fat ain't round here," opined Larry, touching his stomach. "He's got plenty up here too."

He touched his head and Stretch chuckled again. Five minutes later, they were choosing a table at the famous steakhouse and trading greetings with a pretty waitress.

"Steaks," she guessed as they hung up their hats.

"Any way they come, little lady," Larry said genially.

"We're as ready as we'll ever be," grinned Stretch.

Christine, the proprietor's daughter, studied them curiously before retreating to the kitchen.

"First time here?" she asked. "I have

this feeling I've seen you before."

"No," said Larry. "You must be thinkin' of two other hombres."

Renfield and Berman did not descend from the second passenger car until the Dobsons had alighted. A porter had unloaded baggage of travellers staying overnight onto a hand-cart. Other passengers were starting for the Givney Hotel, but the rogues from Sacramento ignored them, concentrating on the young couple.

"They're separating," Berman observed. "She's following passengers to the hotel, he's headed uptown. I'll tag him, while you check us into our rooms. You said they'll take a stagecoach from here, but we'd best be sure."

At this time, Jed and Elmer were dismounting from their badly winded horses in a copse less than a hundred yards south of the railroad tracks and in sight of Bellamy. A stiff pace had been set since they began their journey. Their animals had been spelled, but not as often as necessary, as indicated by their lathered hides, their panting and the layers of dust coating their riders.

"Well, by glory, we made it!" enthused Jed. "Thar she are, pal! Bellamy!"

"It's a wonderment we didn't have to walk the last ten miles," grouched Elmer. "The way you had us push these critters, they're near ready to flop."

"We'll water and feed 'em when they cool down," muttered Jed.

"Jed, even when they've cooled, they ain't totin' us another six feet till they got their strength back."

"Don't fret yourself," grinned Jed. "They'll get plenty rest, on accounts we ain't gonna grab what we're here for till past midnight."

"Better wait that long, huh?"

"Damn right. Gonna be a warm night, so you can count on 'em beddin' down with the window open. That'll make it easy for us." Jed declared his strategy, making it sound absurdly simple. "All we gotta do is get in their room. We pull the shade and, while you light the lamp and keep your gun on 'em' case they wake up, I grab you-know-what."

"Where we gonna find 'em?" demanded Elmer.

"A hotel — where else?" shrugged Jed. "Likely close to the railroad depot. You'll find it easy."

"Me?"

"Right. You're our scout."

"What do I gotta do?"

"What d'you mean — what do you gotta do? Nothin' to it. After we eat, you just sashay into town casual-like, check the hotels, find where them Dodsons're stayin' and, when the clerk ain't lookin', you take a peek at the register, get their room number. Then you find out where the room's at, which window — and we're all set."

"I gotta *walk* in?"

"Smarter that way, pal. A jasper afoot don't get noticed by no lawman as quick as if he rid in."

"And — uh — when we go in to grab the gutcincher?"

"We'll do that on our own feet too."

"I dunno, Jed. I don't like . . . "

"Listen, suppose we gotta make a run for it? On our feet, we'll move quieter. Horses're noisier when it's way after midnight and the town's quiet. Give our position away. On our own two feet, we got a better chance of sneakin' back here and not gettin' spotted."

Though nervous again, Elmer Biddle agreed they should act in accordance with the Kinch strategy.

Hovering by the entrance to the Wells Fargo office, Herb Berman cocked an ear to Pete Dobson's consultation with the ticket clerk. He heard all he needed to hear. The next coach Idaho-bound would depart Bellamy 1 p.m. tomorrow. One way passage for two to Scudder Creek included all meals and accommodation en route.

By the time the young rancher

74

emerged from the stage depot, the eavesdropper was on his way to the hotel.

The Texans, meanwhile, had disposed of their finest steak dinner in many a long year. Billy Morke had not exaggerated; when it came to steaks, the Stendahl touch was magic. They urged Christine to compliment her parents on their behalf when she collected the empty plates.

"I'll do that — and not for the first time," she smiled. "Ready for your pie now?"

"Pie later, right?" Larry suggested to his partner.

"Right," Stretch eagerly agreed.

"Same again, honey," said Larry.

"You want seconds?" she asked incredulously.

"We're storin' up memories," explained Stretch.

"When we leave this town, will we ever again eat such elegant steaks?" challenged Larry. "I wouldn't bet on it — so same again."

The tall men were half-way through their second steaks when another badge-toting, double gunhung Chugg appeared in the restaurant's street doorway, warily surveying the diners, alert for strange faces. To Larry and Stretch, he looked to be almost a replica of the thickset, bushy-browed, beady-eyed man whose suspicion they had aroused at the Four Leaf Clover. Were the Chugg brothers triplets? No. They didn't suppose Deputy Nick had changed his shirt, and this Chugg's shirt was of a different color.

Upon sighting the Texans, he frowned truculently and started for their table.

"Here we go again," Stretch remarked while munching.

"Are they ever gonna learn we ain't the James brothers?" grinned Larry.

The lawman arrived, hovering menacingly, thumbs hooked in shellbelt. They pretended not to notice him till he growled a command.

"Identify yourselves."

Larry raised his eyes and nodded affably.

"We already did," he announced.

"I ain't talked to you jaspers before," countered the lawman.

"You ain't Deputy Mick Chunck that we met at the Four Leaf Clover?" frowned Stretch.

"Name's Chugg," he scowled. "I'm Deputy Rick. That must've been my brother Mick — I mean Nick. Listen, don't mess with our names. We take no sass from saddlebums, us Chuggs. We're the law here and you better not forget it."

"Well," said Larry. "I don't reckon we're apt to forget you."

"Name yourselves," ordered Deputy Rick.

"Be glad to," shrugged Larry. "This here's my friend Mister Woodville Emerson."

"And this here's my friend Mister Lawrence Valentine," offered Stretch.

The beady eyes narrowed to slits.

"Them names're some familiar."

"People keep sayin' that," remarked Larry. "I never could figure why."

"If we hold warrants on you two, you're in real trouble," declared Deputy Rick. He squared his shoulders. "Wanted men spook when they hear of us Chuggs. Ain't no outlaw can escape us, and that goes double for Hamill and his no-good gang."

"Who?" asked Stretch.

"Reno Hamill," Deputy Rick said grimly. "He's on the loose, but not for long. It'll be us Chuggs settle his hash. It's only a matter of time. His days're numbered!"

"We ever hear of Reno Hamill?" Larry asked Stretch.

"Nope," shrugged Stretch. "But we're kind of ignorant, ain't we? I mean, we never heard of the Jug brothers till today."

"Chugg!" thundered the deputy. "Get the name right!" He pointed threateningly. "Now I'm gonna check our records. Meanwhile, don't leave town, hear?"

He turned on his heel and trudged out, after which the taller Texan confided his puzzlement.

"Three of 'em, the barkeep said," he recalled. "It figures the council must've pinned the sheriff's star on the smartest of 'em — but how smart could *he* be?"

"Sometimes you ask the damnedest questions," grinned Larry.

Deputy Rick hurried downtown to the law office. He didn't trip on the threshold, but collided with a chair in his haste to reach the file cabinet. After locating a thick folder, he rummaged through it in hopes of turning up a 'Wanted' dodger adorned by two familiar faces; it didn't occur to him that brother Nick had already done so. Same result. To his chagrin, no warrants on L. Valentine or W. E. Emerson.

"But they're trouble-makers just the same," he assured himself, returning the folder to the files. "So, while I'm on patrol, I'll keep a sharp eye out, be ready to nail 'em soon as they start somethin'."

After supper in the hotel dining room, the Dobsons returned to their room. Kitty had to get to work with needle and thread; her one and only bonnet was in need of repair. Watching her, her husband vowed.

"There'll come a time, honey. We'll be grazing prime beef, a fine herd. There'll be money enough for everything, and the first thing you're gonna have is a pretty new hat."

"Nice thought, Pete darling," she nodded, seating herself by the lamp. "But clothes don't matter. More important things we need, like lumber enough to fix the barn and maybe make the bunkhouse a little bigger. You keep saying it, and I know it's true. By the time we can afford new breed-stock, we'll need to hire extra hands. There'll be too much work for just you and Clem and Shorty."

"It'll all happen, you'll see," he muttered. "If I wasn't sure I could make P-Bar-D grow, I wouldn't have had the nerve to ask you to marry me."

"Heaven knows I was getting impatient," she smiled. "If you hadn't proposed when you did, *I'd* have asked *you*."

"You're joshing me," he grinned.

"No," she assured him. "That's the truth."

"You're the best, Kitty," he said fondly. "If, in my whole life, I only did one wise thing, it was marrying you."

"What will you do before we turn in?" she asked. "Boring for you, just sitting here watching me sew."

"Feel like taking a walk," he said. "Like to stretch my legs. Felt a mite cooped on the train. It'll be worse tomorrow. Depot clerk told me there'll be six of us boarding the coach."

"We'll have to make the most of it," she suggested. "You won't feel so cooped nor impatient if you just keep remembering every mile we travel takes us closer to home." As he rose and reached for his hat, she voiced pleas. "Be careful. We don't know this town and it could be dangerous for strangers. Walk clear of the saloons."

"Nothing's gonna happen," he soothed. "And why would I end up in a saloon? I have to watch our money. We got enough to take us home, but there's no extra for a drink in a bar or playing the games of chance." He moved across to kiss her. "Back in an hour."

When Pete Dobson began his after-supper constitutional, Renfield and Berman were drinking in an uptown saloon, Deputy Rick patrolling and Larry and Stretch paying their tab at Stendahl's.

And two local hard cases, Cayley and Schultz, were on the lookout for an easy mark. Despite the admiration accorded them by the bartender at the Four Leaf Clover, Sheriff Dick Chugg and brothers Nick and Rick had not yet lowered the boom on every felon in their bailiwick. Cayley and Schultz, whose specialty was night-time robbery with violence, were two of several who had evaded the bumptious Chuggs.

When they sighted Pete, they adhered to their regular routine, first scanning the immediate area for any sign of a patrolling lawman, then quickening their step with the intention of jumping their victim when he reached an alleymouth; they worked best in the dark.

"He ain't heeled," Cayley observed.

"Yeah, fine," grinned Schultz. "Makes it easier."

They had sighted no shotgun-toting deputy. Unfortunately for them, they were concentrating on the lone walker, unaware of two tall men who had emerged from Stendahl's Steakhouse a few moments before and were strolling this same side of the street, approaching from the opposite direction.

The Texans were about to fish out Durham sacks to build their after-supper smokes when, dead ahead, they saw the young man seized and hustled into a side alley. An exchange of remarks would have been superfluous; on such occasions, they never paused for discussion, they just acted.

A quarter-way along the dimly lit alley, Pete was shoved against a wall with jarring force. He cursed and raised a hand to defend himself, but not fast enough. After he took a hard blow to the face, a gun was aimed at him.

"Not a yelp outa you," muttered Schultz. "Hand over your wallet — right now — or we'll just bust your skull and help ourselves!"

It wasn't one of Pete Dobson's best moments. His wallet. Probably they'd take his small change too. Every nickel he had and probably the watch that had been his father's, a timepiece of sentimental value — surrendered to these thieving skunks. He was about to take a chance and yell for help. Maybe they'd be reluctant to shoot him, fearing the shot would bring the local law down on them. He was thinking fast, remembering his wife back there in a hotel room, when two more men came bounding into the alley.

"Drop the gun," growled Larry.

Startled, Schultz made two bad mistakes. First, he whirled and squeezed trigger. Second, he fired too fast. At that, the bullet sped between the charging Texans, missing Stretch's left shoulder by less than an inch. Before Schultz could re-cock his weapon, Larry grasped the wrist of his gun-hand and forced it upward. Simultaneously, he slammed his bunched right to Schultz's belly twice and to his jaw once. As for Cayley, he wasn't given time to aim a blow at the taller Texan. Something that felt like a rock mashed his nose and sent him hurtling backward; the mighty left fist of Stretch Emerson, which might as well have *been* a rock.

A block away, Deputy Rick reacted to the echo of the single report. A gunshot! That could mean trouble and, as a deputy sheriff of Bellamy County, it was his duty to investigate. Having figured that out all by himself, he broke into a run and beelined for the source of the sound.

Other sounds reached him as he approached the alleymouth, steady resounding thuds caused by Pete's rescuers bouncing his assailants off the walls either side of the alley. Still fifteen feet away, Rick Chugg jerked to a halt to watch something large fly out of the alley and pitch into the street with an impact that raised dust. Hell's bells — a full-grown man! With his shotgun at the ready, he advanced two more paces, only to halt again. A second human missile hurtled out of the alley to crash beside the first.

'This,' he decided, suddenly inspired, 'is serious!'

He barged on to the alleymouth to reach it just as the tall men emerged, supporting Pete, whose right hand held a handkerchief to his bloody face.

"Gotcha!" the deputy growled triumphantly. "Valentine — Emerson — you're under arrest! Street-fightin's an offense in Bellamy!"

"Which one're you?" Stretch impatiently demanded. "Chick — Wick — who . . . ?"

"Deputy Rick — and none of your smart talk, Emerson!" chided Rick.

"That's the dumbest thing I ever heard a lawman say," scowled Pete. "If it wasn't for these gents, those bastards in the street would've robbed me. They jumped me, shoved me into the alley and put a gun on me. You want to do something useful? Throw those lousy thieves in jail."

"Now wait a minute . . . " began Deputy Rick.

"You ought to be thanking these gents — as I'm thanking them," muttered Pete, "instead of threatening to arrest 'em."

"Now, Slick," lectured Stretch. "A good deputy's just got to learn to tell the good hombres from the bad hombres."

"And quit pointin' that damn cannon at us," Larry said sharply.

Profoundly disappointed, Deputy Rick

pleaded with the victim.

"You sure which two jumped you and which two pulled 'em off of you? Couldn't it be the other way round?"

"You sure you're a lawman?" challenged Pete. "Listen, I'm hurtin', I've had a six-gun shoved in my ribs and my wife'll be worrying about me and I got no more time for your dumb questions."

"Do your duty, Vic," urged Stretch, pointing. "The county jail's thataway."

"Hah! What would *you* know, smart-ass?" Deputy Rick insisted on having the last word. "You're pointin' uptown. The jail's *downtown*."

He trudged to the befuddled and groaning thieves, kicked them till they struggled upright and began marching them downtown. No longer interested in the deputy and his prisoners, Larry drew Pete into the light of the nearest streetlamp and urged him remove the handkerchief.

"Slow, amigo, 'case it's stuck to the wound."

"It's nothing," protested Pete. "Hey, did he call you Valentine and Emerson? I know about you!"

"Yeah, fine, let's see what them sonsabitches did to your face, boy," frowned Larry. The handkerchief was removed. He studied the angry gash and glanced at his partner. "What d'you think?"

"Real mean cut," observed Stretch. "Think it'll need stitchin'?"

"Best play if safe," decided Larry. "We'll take him to a doc."

"No, forget it," mumbled Pete. "It doesn't hurt any more . . . "

"The hell it doesn't," countered Larry.

" . . . and doctors got to be paid," Pete continued, embarrassed now. "Thanks for helping, but no doctor, okay? I'm carrying just enough cash to get Kitty and me home to Scudder Creek and not a dime more."

"Don't fret yourself," soothed Stretch. "We got plenty."

"Whatever it costs, we'll settle with the doc," said Larry. "Listen, you're young, but you ain't foolish. Ever hear of blood poison, infection? Why take chances?" He nodded to his partner. "We need a doc for him."

"Sure," said Stretch, and thrust out a long arm, giving a passer-by no option but to halt in his tracks. Larry growled the question. The local was helpful.

"Doc Tilder's closest. Walk a block down, other side of Main, turn left into Prosser and the Tilder place is the third one along."

"Muchas gracias," nodded Larry. "Let's go, kid."

"This is charity," fretted Pete, as they crossed Main Street.

"Whatsamatter? You never did a kindness for a stranger?" challenged Stretch.

"Well, sure," said Pete.

"Bueno," grunted Larry. "A favor rates a favor, so quit arguin'."

It was not an inconvenient time for the urbane Dr Adam Tilder. He had finished an excellent supper and a good cigar when his housekeeper answered the front doorbell. Emerging from the parlor, he greeted the casualty and escorts and conducted them to his surgery.

The ugly mark on the Pete's left cheek was swabbed and inspected and the medico's verdict was encouraging.

"It won't need stitches, shouldn't leave a scar either. A little antiseptic to counter infection, some balm and a dressing."

"We have to leave tomorrow, Doc," Pete told him. "The one o'clock stage."

"We?" asked Tilder.

"My wife and me," said Pete.

"The lady's quite capable I'm sure," said Tilder. "I can let you have enough of the ointment, some cotton and plaster, for her to change the dressing day after tomorrow. Keep it on another day, then you won't need it any more. Just keep the wound clean and it'll heal soon enough."

"I sure appreciate this, gents," said

Pete. "Seems a lot of trouble for . . . "

"Better this way," insisted Larry.

"Any kind of gash, bullet, knife or fist, got to be patched fast," said Stretch. "We're mighty particular, on account of . . . " He shrugged and looked away. "Never mind."

"Because you and your friend have suffered many such wounds — and worse," the doctor remarked while preparing the dressing. "I believe, if you giants stripped, I'd have difficulty counting your battle-scars — there'd be so many. I recognized you of course."

"Too many do," grouched Larry.

"Larry and Stretch," sighed Tilder. "Nineteenth century knights errant, compulsive nomads, righters of wrongs, seemingly indestructible. I stress *seemingly*, gentlemen. Unlike knights of an earlier era, you wear no armor. You aren't bullet-proof."

"Ain't that the truth," Stretch sadly agreed.

"Our time'll come," shrugged Larry. "Meanwhile, we're alive and kickin' and with plenty to be thankful for." He glanced at Pete. "Leavin' tomorrow, huh?"

"Headed home to our spread outside Scudder Creek," nodded Pete. "It's scarce a spread yet. We're running just fifty head, but give us time and we'll make it. Like I keep telling Kitty, P-Bar-D's gonna grow."

"Northeast — how far?" asked Larry.

"A long ways," said Pete. "It's high country, clean air, good graze. We're north of the Humboldt and east of the Independence Mountains."

The tall men traded wistful grins; they were thinking of an old friend.

"You know a town called Cornerstone?" prodded Stretch.

"Passed through it about four years ago on my way to Scudder Creek," recalled Pete. "Yeah, I didn't see much of the town but, by the time I reached a horse ranch, the JG outfit, I was poorly, got wet to my skin fording the river, had some kind of fever. Two weeks I was laid up at the Gage Place. Jim and his wife and the one they call Ma Dowell, they tended me till I was strong enough to travel on. Great folks. I'm never gonna forget 'em."

"I'll be doggoned." Stretch grinned at his partner. "He's talkin' about Nevada Jim."

"You know Jim Gage?" Pete asked eagerly.

"Old amigo of ours," muttered Larry. "We don't run into him as often as we'd like to."

"Hey, small world!" The young rancher was delighted.

"All finished," announced Tilder. He slipped a few items into a paper sack and stowed it in the patient's coat pocket. "A little of the ointment and everything your wife'll need to replace the dressing."

The doctor was paid, thanked and farewelled. Pete's spirits were high when they left the Tilder house to walk back to Main Street. He was oblivious to the dressing plastered to his face, so great was his pleasure at meeting friends of a benefactor he had never forgotten.

"Wait till I tell Kitty I ran into a couple of friends of Jim Gage," he enthused. "She never met him, but I've talked of him so much it's like she knows him too."

"How're you feelin' now, Pete?" asked Larry. "Steady on your feet? You lost some blood."

"Feel fine," Pete assured him. "Listen, how about you come on back to the hotel and meet the wife? We're overnighting at the Givney Hotel."

"Us too," said Stretch. "Room Four."

"We're in Eight," grinned Pete. "So what do you say? We can talk of Jim and . . ." He suddenly remembered the circumstances of their meeting and raised a hand to his face. "Hey, you'll *have* to stick with me — help me convince Kitty it wasn't my fault what happened to me. Last thing she said before I walked out was be careful."

"You sure it'll be okay?" frowned Larry.

95

"At first sight, some women get leery of us," explained Stretch. "Damned if I savvy why. Couple harmless hombres like us."

"You beat hell out of those jaspers who jumped me," chuckled Pete. "I got to say you didn't look harmless when you were heaving 'em out of the alley. But don't worry about Kitty. Any friends of mine're friends of hers."

"Well," said Larry. "Maybe just long enough to ease her mind — 'case she thinks it was a bullet tore your face."

A few minutes after they reached Main Street and turned right to move on to the hotel, they were accosted by a shotgun-toting lawman who demanded they accompany him to the sheriff's office.

"It's Wick again," frowned Stretch.

"No, this'un's Vic," said Larry.

"I'm Deputy Rick," scowled the lawman. "We identified them robbers and Dick — my brother the sheriff — says we're gonna hold 'em for trial. So we gotta have a statement from the victim and . . . " He stared hard at the tall men, "you hot shots that horned in."

"Horned in and saved my bankroll," growled Pete. "What there is of it."

"You're comin' with me," insisted Deputy Rick. "And I mean right now."

"I guess it's okay, runt," suggested Stretch. "They can't lock us up for helpin' Pete and discouragin' a couple hard cases."

"Sure," shrugged Larry. "It can't do no harm to help these Chubbs. Seems to me . . . "

"Chuggs!" corrected the deputy.

"Seems to me," Larry continued, "they're the kind of lawmen need all the help they can get."

And so, escorted by Deputy Rick, Pete and his rescuers walked downtown to the sheriff's office fronting the county jail, Pete pleased to observe it was only a short distance from the Givney Hotel.

The Texans showed no surprise that the hefty boss-lawman filling the chair behind the desk was bushy-browed, beady-eyed and, in every way, a third edition of Deputies Rick and Nick.

"You're the transient near got robbed." Sheriff Dick Chugg said this almost accusingly as he eyed Pete. "Let's start with your name, boy."

"Peter Durand Dobson," Pete informed him. "P-Bar-D ranch out of Scudder Creek, Northeast Nevada. Room Eight, Givney Hotel. Leaving on tomorrow's stage." He helped himself to a chair. "If you want this in writing, I'll need pen and ink and paper."

# 4

## It Takes All Kinds

EAGER to be out of here and back with his wife, the young rancher inked a pen, reached for a pad and began writing, while the Chuggs glowered at the Texans, resenting their indifference; Larry was studying the wall map right of the gunrack, Stretch lounging at a front window, boredly scanning Main Street.

"So you're Valentine and Emerson," growled Sheriff Dick, "that think they're smarter's any lawmen."

"Depends which lawmen you're speakin' of," Larry drawled without turning his head.

"Already got brother Nick's report on you," the sheriff warned. "You claim you only drifted in to try Stendahl's steaks."

"And that's the pure truth, Sheriff suh," yawned Stretch. "We sure didn't plan on tangling with a couple no-account hard cases."

"Didn't believe a man could get robbed in Bellamy," remarked Larry. "Barkeep at the Four Leaf Clover guaranteed you Jugs run this town good, got all the lowdowns spooked."

"We're the Chuggs, not the Jugs!" boomed Sheriff Dick. "And *look* at me while I'm talkin' to you!"

"Why?" asked Stretch. "We already seen you."

"Be with you in a minute," soothed Larry. "Right fine map. Shows the Cornerstone County area way north-east. We got a good buddy up thataway."

Pete made short work of his statement. The sheriff read it, ordered Pete to sign it and added his own signature as witness. Then he glowered at the tall men again and sourly enquired,

"Can either of you smart-asses write?"

"Yep," grunted Larry.

"Both of us," said Stretch. "But my partner's volunteerin'."

"Sure," said Larry. "It might's well be me." After which he turned away from the wall map, took the chair vacated by Pete and paused with the pen held over the pad, matching stares with the sheriff. "But — uh — maybe this'll be a waste of time."

"What d'you mean?" challenged Sheriff Dick.

"I know I can write," frowned Larry. "Question is — can you read?"

Both brothers seethed. Stretch kept his gaze averted. Pete covered a grin with his hand.

"Listen, Valentine . . . !" roared the sheriff.

"Forget it," grinned Larry. "Joke. You can quit boilin'. This'll only take a minute."

He inked the pen and, ignoring the venomous glares of the brothers, wrote clearly and concisely for what seemed only a few moments. Then he added his signature and snapped his fingers. Stretch yawned again, loafed from the window to the desk, accepted the inked pen from his partner and added his name to the statement, which was then nudged across the desk for Sheriff Dick's inspection. The boss-lawman was at once critical.

"Call this a statement?"

"Read it out loud," urged Larry. "It says it all. What d'you want? Frills?"

The sheriff read aloud,

"We saw two slobs grab Pete Dobson and shove him into an alley. One of them took a shot at us when we hustled in there. Then we clobbered them and threw them in the street for the deputy to collect. Yours truly, L. Valentine and W. E. Emerson."

"He reads real good, runt," remarked Stretch.

"Got every word right," approved Larry. "Not one mistake."

"I guess that's enough, Dick," mumbled Rick. "We got Cayley and Schultz cold. Circuit judge'll rule 'em guilty, betcha boots."

"All right, all right," grimaced Sheriff Dick, as Larry got to his feet. "But I'm warnin' you smartasses. 'Tween now and when you ride outa my bailiwick, you damn well better keep your noses clean."

"C'mon now, how could we run into another hassle?" shrugged Stretch. "We'll be on our way right after breakfast. Meantime, all we're gonna do is visit with Pete and his wife and then turn in and get our sleep."

"Is there a badge-toter any place that'll believe we're peaceable?" wondered Larry.

"Don't seem so, runt," Stretch said regretfully.

"And somethin' else you better not forget," growled Deputy Rick. "It's gonna be us Chuggs round up the Hamill gang, not you damn show-offs."

"Heed what my brother's tellin' you, Valentine," ordered the sheriff. "I don't care spit for all that hogwash about the Pinkertons tryin' to hire you. In my territory, you're just another no-account saddlebum and you don't play detective, savvy? The law, meanin' me and my brothers, gonna stop them bandits. Not you and your scrawny sidekick."

"I'm sure glad to hear that," Larry warmly declared.

"Me too," nodded Stretch. "Does my heart good. Gives me a warm feelin' right here." He held hand to heart. "On account of we've had our bellyful of tradin' lead with bandidos. Am I lyin', runt?"

"You ain't lyin'," said Larry. "Sheriff, you and Slick and Mick're welcome to Hamill and every other badman you can nail. All we want is to mind our own blame business."

"Kitty'll be fretting," pleaded Pete. "You through with us, Sheriff?"

"Must be," insisted Larry, starting for the door. "Because we're sure as hell through with him."

"Nice talkin' to you do-right

Chunks — 'scuse me — Chuggs," drawled Stretch.

"It's been a pleasure," Larry called over his shoulder. "We really mean that."

Outside the Chugg headquarters, crossing toward the hotel, Pete began chuckling.

"I didn't enjoy what those hold-up artists did to me," he grinned. "But meeting the Texas Trouble-Shooters makes it worthwhile. The way you sassed those big-mouth lawmen — I'm still laughing."

"They ain't all the same, Pete," Larry assured him.

"There's lawmen we plumb admire," drawled Stretch. "But then — uh — there's lawmen like the Glugs — or whatever they call 'emselves."

Entering the lobby, the tall men collected their key and followed Pete upstairs and along the corridor to Room 8. Pete knocked and, when his wife answered, asked,

"You still dressed, honey? I got a

105

couple friends out here, like you to meet 'em."

Good timing. Kitty had intended changing to her sleeping nightgown a few minutes from now. She opened the door and, for a shocked moment, had eyes only for her husband.

"Pete! Your face!"

"Everything's fine, don't give it a thought." He ushered the Texans in, closed the door and performed introductions. "Want me to say those names again, sweetheart? Larry and Stretch!"

The trouble-shooters towered over her, heads bared, hats held to chests. She stared up at them and decided,

"Well now, it couldn't have been *them* you were fighting with. More than your poor face'd be hurt. You'd have been carried in on a stretcher."

"Let me tell her what happened," Pete begged his new friends, gesturing them to the room's only chairs. He sat with Kitty on the near edge of the bed, held her hand and briefly recounted

106

his misadventure, stressing their money was safe and his injury minor. In conclusion, he cheerily opined, "Those thieves'll be hurting for a week. You should've seen how Larry and Stretch beat the tar out of 'em."

"No, you shouldn't have, Mrs Dobson ma'am," Larry assured her. "It wasn't a fittin' sight for a lady."

"Don't Mrs Dobson ma'am me," she chided, and the drifters decided they liked her smile. "After all you've done, and it means so much to us, I'll thank you to call me Kitty."

"Like I told you," Pete reminded them. "We got just enough to take us home. If those thieving coyotes had gotten away with my wallet . . . "

"Oh, Lord," sighed Kitty. "We'd have been stranded here — with not a cent."

"Glad to do it," Stretch declared with an amiable grin. "We're special glad since Pete said he's a friend of a friend of ours."

"They're old buddies of Nevada Jim,

honey," grinned Pete. "Remember I told you about the time I was down with a fever at a horse ranch?"

"Mister Gage is another I'm beholden to," she nodded, "though I haven't even met him." She surveyed their guests in honest puzzlement. "Only one thing I don't understand about you, Larry, and you, Stretch. I was knee-high first time I heard tales of you and I remember newspaper pictures. Now I'm a grown woman and I look it and that's as should be — so how can it be that you look no older than when I was a little girl?"

"You know, runt, that's a plumb reasonable question," frowned Stretch.

"Sure it is," shrugged Larry. "But I got no answer for Kitty, because I don't savvy it neither."

"They're in Number Four just along the hall," offered Pete.

"That's nice," she frowned. "But not as important as where they were when you were set on."

"I was lucky, and don't I know

108

it," he said fervently. "Seems they walked out of a diner a little way ahead just in time — right when I most needed help." To the Texans he remarked, "From here to Scudder Creek, I won't be fool enough to leave my gun in my valise. I'll be packing it when we board the stage tomorrow."

"How long are you staying here?" asked Kitty.

"We'll be movin' on right after breakfast," said Larry.

"We could get together again for breakfast," suggested Pete.

"Our pleasure," said Larry.

"But then you'll be leaving and we'll never see you again," complained Kitty. "That's a shame."

The tall men relaxed and conversation flowed easily. A casual enquiry as to how the Dobsons happened to be so far from home led to discussion of the famous Sierra Stash. Both drifters had heard of it, and who hadn't? Be it fact or rumor, the late Clute Marchmount's buried gold rated with the Comstock Lode.

"So you're kin to them Marchmounts?" prodded Stretch.

"Youngest relative of Aunt Ellie," nodded Kitty. "Well, youngest adult relative. My cousins Brad and Sam are married and have children."

"Kitty's still a mite disappointed," offered Pete. "We travelled a long way for the will reading. I keep telling her it doesn't matter she inherited no cash. It would've been useful, but we've kept the spread going up till now and we'll go on doing that."

"Long journey for nothin'," Larry sympathized.

"Well," said Pete, "not exactly nothing. She did get something."

"Pete," frowned Kitty.

"Begging your pardon, honey," he grinned. For the Texans' benefit, he explained, "It was something personal."

"Sure," shrugged Larry. "Sacramento, huh? I guess it's plenty big, bein' the state capital."

"Beautiful city," remarked Kitty. "But we'll be glad to see Scudder Creek again. Hometown folks're friendlier." The guests were touched by the compassion in her eyes. "It's sad to think that, wandering all the time, you don't know how it feels to have a hometown."

"I'll bet a lot of people have asked why you couldn't settle down," said Pete.

"They keep askin'," shrugged Stretch. "What can we tell 'em?"

"Just one of those things," muttered Larry. "We're the kind has to keep movin'." Intrigued, he steered the talk back to the old legend. "Old Clute's stash, *no* Marchmount inherits it?"

"Wasn't a word about it in the will," said Pete.

"Anyway, who'd know how to find it?" wondered Stretch. "Been many a long year since the old feller went prospectin'. Maybe even *he* couldn't've found his way back to it."

"Hard to remember," opined Larry,

"after so long a time."

"Kitty's other cousins figure there has to be a map," said Pete. "If there is, nobody's ever seen it."

"I guess, when he got to be so rich, it didn't matter to him no more," Stretch supposed. "Aw, well . . . " He grinned at his partner. "Wouldn't make no never-mind to the likes of us. Gettin' rich is just what we never craved."

"Right," agreed Larry. "Hunger for a fortune and you could be a sad hombre your whole life. Better to be thankful for what you got."

The visit lasted another hour. Bidding the young couple goodnight, moving along to their own room, the drifters were mutually agreed they would be more than ready to quit Bellamy next morning. Nothing for them here. Meeting and getting to know the Dobsons had been pleasant and supper at Stendahl's had been everything Billy Morke predicted, but Bellamy no doubt had a newspaper and, sooner or later, its editor would pick up word of the attempted robbing of a transient and the decisive thwarting of the robbers by a couple of well-known trouble-shooters. If Bellamy's newspaperman were in accord with others of his profession, and he probably was, he would make capital of the incident, blow it up to a front page story. More publicity for Larry and Stretch. And did they need it? Like a boil on the butt they needed it.

Stretch chose a bed and flopped. Larry, squatting on the other bed, suggested he should rise at least long enough to remove his boots and unstrap his Colts.

"Else you're apt to doze off and, if you sleep on your side, you'll wonder why your hip hurts come sun-up."

The taller Texan inspected skinned knuckles while peeling down to his Long Johns.

"Another town, another fight," he grouched.

"We had two choices," Larry pointed out. "Pretend we didn't see what we saw — or do somethin' about it."

In another room on this floor of the hotel, Renfield and Berman planned an after midnight break-in.

"Mightn't have to break in at all," Berman predicted, mopping his brow. "Hot for the time of year. Chances are they'll leave their window open, so all we have to do is climb out of here, sneak along the gallery — and get it." He took pieces of black cloth from his carpetbag and tossed one to Renfield. "You'll need that, just in case one of 'em wakes and sees us."

Renfield tried the hood on for size; he could see clearly through the eyeholes.

"We'll look fearsome," he remarked. "If that dumb cousin of mine catches sight of us, she'll scream bloody murder."

"Have a kerchief ready," urged Berman. "Better to gag her, and fast, than let her tip our hand. As for her man, leave him to me." He drew his Smith & Wesson .38 and grinned coldly. "A rap on his skull and he'll go right back to sleep."

"We ought to wait till around one-thirty," suggested Renfield, consulting his watch.

"Might be too early," countered Berman. "Two o'clock sounds safer to me."

"Fine," nodded Renfield. "At two we make our play."

Twenty minutes after midnight, when Elmer Biddle entered town from the south, he managed to do so without arousing the curiosity of the patrolling deputy, Nick Chugg. With Elmer, this was instinctive, he having a professional aversion to law officers of every type.

The night-clerk of the hotel nearest the railroad depot, Givney's, was snoring in a padded chair behind the reception desk when the pudgy felon sneaked into the lobby. Elmer was able to inspect the register undetected. Names, signatures — why in hell did people who wrote clearly most times make such a scrawl when it came to signing their names? The clerk grunted and, fearing he would open his eyes, Elmer did his checking in haste.

"That'll be them," he assured himself, making a mental note of a room number.

More checking now. He had to climb the stairs quietly, seek the room, then creep out again and, from the side alley, count windows and make certain of the location of the sleeping Dobsons.

He walked out of Bellamy as unobtrusively as he had walked in. Finding his way back to the copse and his waiting sidekick was not difficult, though he was a trifle footsore when he got there.

"Find out what we need to know?" Jed asked urgently.

"That's what you told me to do, dincha?" grouched Elmer. "We'll do good. I got their room spotted. What we gotta hope for is them firestairs don't creak when we climb up to the gallery."

"We'll pussyfoot it real sneaky,"

enthused Jed. "Hey, this is gonna be a cinch!"

"I guess so," frowned Elmer. "But I gotta tell you, Jed, my gut'll feel a whole lot steadier when we get back to here with that consarn corset thing, shove it in a saddlebag and head west for the ol' Sierra Nevada."

"Sure, we got plenty time later for hackin' up the corset and gettin' the map," nodded Jed. "Important thing, after our big coup, is get the hell outa this territory. And there ain't nothin' can stop us, pal. By the time we're ridin', our critters'll be fresh and rarin' to go."

When they estimated the time was right, they broke from the timber and made for Bellamy's near side. Jed's feet hurt when they reached the alley paralleling Main. From there, they made for the shorter alley west of the hotel. After entering it, they paused, both staring up to the gallery.

"Which one?" demanded Jed.

"Third window from this corner,"

mumbled Elmer. "No, that ain't right. Third from the front corner."

"Make up your damn mind!"

"Don't rush me — I'm thinkin'."

"Think fast!"

"I got it. Third window from this end. And, hey look, it's half-open!"

"Gonna be full open in a couple seconds. Now, 'fore we climb them stairs, you know what you gotta do?"

"I find the lamp and light it, point my iron at 'em. You find the belly-squeezer, then we get the hell outa there."

"Can't you remember *nothin'*?"

"What'd I forget?"

"Try thinkin' again."

"Oh, sure. We gotta muzzle 'em, leave 'em hogtied with the sheets, so they can't holler and louse up our getaway."

"Now you got it. Here we go, pal."

They drew their bandanas up to their eyes, moved to the stairs and began climbing. Reaching the gallery, they made for the half-open window. Jed hooked his hands under it, raised it as high as it would go and clambered in with Elmer following. They thought to lower the shade before Elmer scratched a match. By its flickering light, he spotted the lamp and made for it, succeeding in reaching it without falling over a chair. Another match was used to touch flame to wick.

Yellow light filled the room, revealing the double bed and nought but the tops of the occupants' heads. Elmer drew his Colt and glanced at Jed, who was pointing triumphantly. Draped over a chairback left of the bed was the prize they sought. Yes siree, a corset, nothing surer.

Jed moved to the chair, began lifting the corset and, at that moment, Elmer sneezed and, for some little time thereafter, it seemed everything that could go wrong went wrong.

One of the sleepers, female and sizeable, raised her head, opened her eyes, gawked at the intruders and loosed a scream that near fractured Elmer's eardrums. The other sleeper, male with wispy grey hair, jerked half-upright, whisked a six-shooter from under his pillow and bellowed,

"Drop that corset and reach for the ceiling!"

"Underwear thieves!" whooped the big woman. "Degenerates!"

Her husband cocked and triggered. The bullet blew a hole through the window shade and, impatiently, he mumbled.

"Where in tarnation're my eyeglasses? I can't see clear without 'em."

With Jed hauling on the corset, a hook of which had snagged to the padding of the chairback, Elmer desperately returned fire. His bullet cannoned off a metal knob of the bedhead, ricocheted and tore his partner's sleeve. Jed yelped, lost his grip of the corset and charged to the window and so did Elmer; escape was all they could think of now. The woman's husband fired in what he believed was their direction; this time he bored a hole in the wall four feet to the right of the window, where the frustrated burglars had jerked the shade free and were struggling to extricate themselves from it.

The din of shooting was more than enough to start Larry and Stretch rolling from their beds, pulling on pants and arming themselves.

Renfield and Berman had been about to climb out their window when the first shot was heard. They swore luridly.

"The hell with it!" breathed Berman. "This will bring the law — fast!"

"What are we going to . . . ?"

"Shut the window, damn it. We have to hide these hoods and change to our nightshirts before a tin badge gets here."

When the Texans dived through their window to land on the gallery, they heard the marauders and glimpsed them disappearing around a corner. Guns at the ready, they yelled a challenge, leapt to their feet and took off in pursuit. As they rounded the corner, they heard booted feet clattering on the firestairs.

"Let's go," growled Larry.

Hustling along to the stairs, they spotted the fleeing men again, in the side alley now and making for its rear end. They were dim targets, but both Texans cut loose anyway and, with .45 slugs coming dangerously close, putting the fear of hell into them, the inept felons took to their heels. Jed was running fast, and still Elmer passed him.

"Missed 'em!" Stretch felt cheated. "And we can't chase the sonsaguns!"

"Barefoot?" winced Larry. "Hell, no."

And he balanced on one foot to pluck a splinter from the other, while Deputy Nick charged along Main, the clamor of gunfire having reached him two blocks away. As the Texans returned to their room, the upstairs corridor was filling with startled guests. Opening their door, the tall men didn't hesitate to show themselves; barefoot and shirtless they were but, on their standards, Levis and the top halves of their underwear made them more presentable than nightshirted overnighters. The Dobsons peered out from their open doorway. Givney and the night-clerk were on hand, trying to calm a couple of apprehensive spinsters. By the time the deputy came bounding up the stairs to demand explanations, the big woman was recounting the outrage to one and all — loudly — her husband still hefting his pistol, but seeing clear now; he had finally located his spectacles.

"You two again!" Deputy Nick scowled at the tall man, as they thrust their Colts into their waistbands.

"It wasn't them!" boomed the big woman.

"Two other jaspers," growled her husband.

"One at a time," ordered the deputy.

123

"Our name is Dawson and we're booked on tomorrow's stage," announced the big woman.

"She's Iris, I'm Phineas," offered Dawson. "The light woke us. They lit our lamp, and one of 'em sneezed."

"It was ghastly!" cried Iris Dawson. "They were degenerates!"

"Tried to steal Iris's corset, by damn," complained Dawson. "Lucky I had this under my pillow."

"Don't point that gun at me," chided Deputy Nick. I'm an officer of the law."

"Did I point it at him?" Dawson asked his wife.

"Phineas valiantly protected me — and my underwear," declared Iris.

"I'd have downed both the skunks if I'd had my eye-glasses," asserted Dawson.

"They grabbed your — uh . . . ?" began Deputy Nick.

"Corset!" snapped Iris.

"Merciful heavens!" gasped one of the spinsters. "What kind of fiend would stoop so low, Eleanor?"

"I just hate to think," fretted the other spinster.

"Sure it wasn't them?" challenged Deputy Nick, glaring at the Texans.

Fearsome in her tent-like nightgown, Iris Dawson became abusive.

"Of course we're sure, you dolt! They were smaller men, much smaller, but I was terrified — and indignant! Fortunately they were craven cowards. When my Phineas began shooting, they fled."

"Didn't look anything like those fellers," said Dawson, after a brief glance at the drifters.

Renfield and Berman were watching from their doorway, as curious as everybody else.

"You're wastin' time, Chick," chided Stretch. "'Stead of lingerin' up here, you ought to be out chasin' 'em."

"What were you doin' when it happened?" demanded Deputy Nick.

"Sleepin', till the shots roused us," said Larry. "Then we pulled on our pants, grabbed our hoglegs and hustled out to the gallery. We took a couple shots at 'em but, by then, they'd made it to the side alley and were hightailin' it."

"Thataway," offered Stretch, pointing.

"We'll run 'em to ground," Deputy Nick assured everybody as he made for the stairs. "No thief can escape the Chuggs!"

"You folks ought to get back to your beds," urged the hotel-keeper. "I apologize for the disturbance, not that it was any fault of the management."

"Nothing like this *ever* happened in Bellamy," the shocked night-clerk assured the guests.

The Texans traded nods with the Dobsons and withdrew into their room. As they returned to their beds, a mystified Stretch complained,

"Thieves ain't what they used to be. What kind of bandido'd want to steal a female's thingummyjig?"

"My hunch is the Dawsons went off half-cocked," said Larry. "Thieves bust into hotel rooms for cash or a gold watch, like them galoots that jumped Pete Dobson. Or a woman's jewellry maybe. But her duds, a petticoat, a doggone corset? Hell, no. Not so you'd notice."

The taller Texan yawned, offered a hunch of his own and won his partner's keen interest.

"So maybe that Dawson gent's packin' a fat bankroll and he's been flashin' it around careless and that's what they were after."

"The Dawsons'll be on that stage tomorrow," frowned Larry.

"Sure," nodded Stretch. "Pete and Kitty too." Sensing Larry's disquiet, he propped himself up on an elbow. "Why? Somethin' botherin' you?"

"Maybe the Chuggs'll run 'em to ground and maybe they won't," muttered Larry. "The Bellamy councilmen figure them brothers're the smartest badge-toters in all Nevada but, for my money, they're dumbheads. And what happens after the stage quits Bellamy?

127

The Dawsons only spotted two marauders . . . "

"That's how many *we* spotted," recalled Stretch.

" . . . but there could be more of 'em," opined Larry.

"Hey now," said Stretch.

"If they want Dawson's dinero bad enough, that Wells Fargo rig could travel far clear of the county line and smack-dab into a hold-up," declared Larry. "Pete and Kitty'll be aboard and Pete'll be heeled. Might be gunplay. Passengers could be in bad trouble."

"I'm readin' your mind," said Stretch. "We got nothin' better to do. Stage don't leave till after lunch so, if we ride out after breakfast . . . "

"Northeast," nodded Larry. "We could scout the stage trail, maybe cut sign of an ambush party." Grimly, he insisted, "The only good ambush is the one you stop before it can happen."

"I'm with you," said Stretch. "Okay if we catch some shut-eye now?"

In another room, other concerned

parties were coming to a decision.

"Who could they be?" Renfield was wondering. "I don't like the coincidence, Herb. Two sneak-thieves break into a room to grab a corset?"

"The wrong room," mused Berman.

"All right, the wrong room, so maybe they aren't too bright," growled Renfield. "But, whoever they are, they've guessed about the map. If they'd gotten into the Dobson's room, it'd be goodbye to our plans."

"There's always another plan, and I just thought of one," said Berman. "We have to forget about trying for the map here. Thanks to those jackasses, the law'll keep the hotel under observation the rest of the night, so we're gonna have to travel, leave around sun-up and find a stakeout somewhere along the Wells Fargo route. Coach doesn't roll till one o'clock, so we'll have ample time to ride far clear of this territory and choose our position."

"We're gonna hold up the stage?" frowned Renfield.

"It's not all that difficult, friend," drawled Berman. "Take it from one who knows, an old hand."

"Early start?" prodded Renfield.

"We check out of here, wake up a horse trader and buy everything we need, including provisions," Berman told him. "We'll be laying out more of our cash, but in a good cause."

"Can just two of us swing this?" challenged Renfield.

"Pushover — if we do it right," grinned Berman. "The hostage trick, it never fails. One of us puts his gun to the head of the driver or guard or maybe a passenger. The hostage gets to be dead in a hurry if the Dobson woman doesn't strip damn quick and hand over what we need. Don't worry, it'll work."

"Whatever you say," muttered Renfield. "But I'd be easier of mind if I knew who they were — those lamebrains who broke into the wrong room."

# 5

## Ambush Fever

THOSE lamebrains who broke into the wrong room eluded the search party recruited by Deputy Nick Chugg for two good reasons.

First reason: Jed and Elmer didn't stop running till they reached the copse where their horses waited. Though badly winded, footsore also and severely shaken, they made short work of readying their mounts, after which they rode a wide half-circle around the county seat and on to the northeast.

Second reason: It took Deputy Nick some considerable time to rouse from sleep the men of his choice, organize horses and weapons and get his search under way in pitch darkness; not till sun-up would they be able to search for tracks of the would-be underwear purloiners.

Jed didn't start cussing until he and Elmer were joining the stage trail.

"You loused it all up!" he berated his disgruntled accomplice. "That bull-voiced old sow couldn't be the Dobson gal! You blame well led us inta the wrong damn room and near got our heads blowed off!"

"Checked the register, didn't I?" grouched Elmer. "Found the room number . . ."

But the *wrong room*!" raged Jed.

"Quit hollerin' at me. Anybody can make a mistake."

"Specially you!"

"Well, I dunno how it all went wrong."

"You done failed me, Elmer. Sure, you checked the register, but you didn't get the right room number, consarn you."

"Listen, it ain't easy. I thought sure the name I read was Dobson and now I savvy how I got tricked. The big female and her trigger-happy man, they must have a name kinda like the Dobson's, so I took it for Dobson. Hell, Jed. you could've made the same mistake. Folks oughta write clearer when they sign their monikers." It now occurred to Elmer to enquire, "Where we headed?"

"This here's the stage trail," growled Jed. "We're gonna find us a place to hide. Then we're gonna hold up the stage and make the Dobson woman hand over what we're after."

"I got a question," frowned Elmer.

"I don't wanta hear it," retorted Jed. "Done made up my mind."

"How do we know the Dobsons'll be on the stage?" demanded Elmer. "Come in on the train, didn't they? So why couldn't they be on that east-bound again tomorrer?"

"Can't you remember *nothin'*?" scowled Jed. "Didn't I tell you what I heard them dudes talkin' about back in Sacramento? The Dobsons gotta switch to the stage in Bellamy on accounta

Dobson's got a spread somewheres way northeast. So they *gotta* be on the stage."

"Oh," said Elmer.

They rode on, both as determined as ever. Their Bellamy reversal had been somewhat intimidating, but they would regain their courage. For a chance at the Sierra Stash, that rich prize, they would stop at nothing.

Well, almost.

After an early breakfast, the Texans were quitting the dining room just as the Dobsons descended to the lobby. The young couple expressed disappointment that their new friends had breakfasted so early, explaining the early morning fracas had caused them to sleep late. Larry explained the excitement had the reverse effect on them.

"We roused early, Stretch was hungry, so we came on down. But maybe this is just hasta la vista, not adios. We plan on headin' northeast."

"So you never can tell," nodded

Stretch. "Might be we'll meet up with you again."

"I certainly hope so," smiled Kitty. "And I thank you again for what you did for Pete."

"So does Pete," grinned her husband, offering his hand.

As they shook, Larry studied the dressing covering half of the young rancher's face. Pete assured him he was in no pain. Larry then noticed the butt of the Colt holstered at Pete's left side, just visible under his open coat, the butt jutting forward. He and Stretch expressed approval. Pete assured them last night's experience had taught him a lesson.

"You got a point," remarked Stretch. "Chances are them heroes wouldn't have jumped you if they'd know you were packin' iron."

The farewell was amiable. And then, unaware two other guests had checked out long before breakfast-time, the drifters purchased a few necessaries at an early opening store and moved on to the livery stable. There, they saddled up, secured saddlebags, packrolls and sheathed rifles, paid the stablehand and got mounted.

It was perhaps fortunate that, making for the stage route, they did not encounter Deputy Nick's posse. One or both of them might have been tempted to offer Nick a few pointers on the art of reading sign, an offer no Chugg would have appreciated.

The eastbound train departed on schedule and, when they next entered the dining room at Givney's the Dobsons' baggage was being collected by a Wells Fargo porter in the lobby, theirs and the grips and carpetbags of passengers with whom they would travel part of the way to their destination. It was a few minutes before noon now. The stage had arrived seven minutes early to put off five travellers, two locals, three who'd be waiting for the next train.

As was their usual routine, driver Harp Malone and his close cohort, shotgun guard Joe Britt, had their lunch at Givney's and, while eating, sized up the half-dozen passengers boarding here.

"Two for Tealsburg, two for Arnold City and two for Scudder Creek," beefy Malone mumbled to wiry Britt. "The two for Scudder Creek'll be with us the longest time."

"They all look like regular folks, but I could wish we weren't haulin' four females out of Bellamy," grouched Britt, a confirmed misogynist.

"Women ain't no trouble," shrugged Malone. "Long as a man don't do somethin' loco — such as marryin' 'em."

It was easy for the stage crew to identify their passengers. At this hotel, it was customary to seat travellers at a table for six if they were booked on the same coach; a chance for people to get acquainted before boarding.

Before any of her companions could start a conversation, big Iris Dawson insisted on recounting her 'horrifying' ordeal in the wee small hours, the intrusion of two blackguards bent on stealing her corset.

"And, but for dear Phineas's prompt action, those depraved roughnecks might have succeeded!" she declared.

"Dear me," said Abigail Dudley.

"How terrible," sympathized her sister Eleanor.

Pete and Kitty politely concealed their amused reaction to Mrs Dawson's harrowing tale. As yet, the significance of the incident, the fact that Pete's and Mr Dawson's signatures could have confused an underwear thief, had not occurred to them.

Tiring of the fascinating subject of his wife's corset, Phineas named Arnold City as their destination, adding he ran a general store there and was returning with his Iris from settling some business with a Virginia City warehouse. Pete responded by informing their fellow-passengers that he and his wife were headed home to their small ranch outside Scudder Creek.

"Oh, well, my sister and I are homebound for Tealsburg," Abigail Dudley announced. "We always take our annual vacation together, and always in California."

"Leppington's Ford on the Sacramento River," smiled Eleanor. "Such a lovely place."

"I've heard of it," said Kitty. "Very popular."

"You ladies in business at Tealsburg?" asked Dawson.

"I'm in charge of the public library," said Abigail. "Eleanor teaches at the community school. It's a nice quiet town."

"I declare, there's so little trouble at Tealsburg, our town marshal and his deputy have practically nothing to do," said Eleanor.

"Too bad all Nevada towns aren't like Tealsburg," commented Pete.

"Your poor face, Mister Dobson," frowned Abigail.

"Just a scratch," frowned Pete. "It'll heal fast enough. Things would've been worse for Kitty and me if those no-goods had gotten my wallet. Lucky for me a couple friends helped me out."

"Those tall fellers, huh?" prodded Dawson. "Same two bucks chased off those other thieves last night. Proves a man needs to stay armed on a long trip."

Harp Malone was grouching again when he started on his coffee.

"Two years," he complained to his partner. "And they still ride free."

"Hamill's bunch." Britt scowled ferociously. "Nevada law's plumb lazy if you ask me. Should've been a posse rounded up them buzzards long before now."

"Too much country to cover, that's the hell of it," said Malone. "They're never gonna catch 'em 'less they can find Hamill's hideout, and he covers his backtrail too good."

"Sometimes it's a lonesome feelin'," mumbled Britt.

"What?" frowned Malone.

"Squattin' up there nursin' a shotgun — I'm an easy target."

"How could you be lonesome? I'm right up here beside of you."

"Sure, Harp, but you got your hands full keepin' three spans movin' along steady. Me, I'm a sittin' duck."

"You've been shot at before."

"Right. And it don't pleasure me none."

While lingering over their coffee, the veterans brooded on the danger endured by other crews of other stage-lines, drivers and guards slain or wounded by raiding parties of the kind led by the notorious Reno Hamill, a desperado destined for listing in the hall of infamy of Nevada outlaws. Malone and Britt weren't demoralized. Defiant was the word. Unlike most stage drivers, Malone packed a .45 rammed into his pants, the butt concealed by his jacket. And Britt was giving serious consideration nowadays to the idea of a spare weapon within easy reach; after all, a shotgun held only two cartridges.

At 12.55 p.m. the driver rose and called to the passengers.

"Better finish up, folks. We're near ready to roll."

The travellers filed out of the dining room after the crew, trading goodbyes with the hotel-keeper and his clerk. Across Main Street they walked to the waiting coach, its fresh team in harness, baggage secured to the roof. As they boarded, Britt annouced.

"Next stop Bald Rock Way Station. We overnight there."

"Excellent meals at Bald Rock," Abigail Dudley enthused, while Pete and Dawson were helping the ladies into the vehicle.

"And the accommodation leaves nothing to be desired," murmured her sister.

Right on time, the coach departed for the northeast run.

The Texans, meanwhile, were quitting the trail some three miles beyond the Bellamy County border to travel the left side of a long line of screening brush. This way, they could follow the trail unseen.

Farther ahead, Renfield and Berman sat their mounts behind high boulders to the right of the trail, already wearing their hoods.

Not as far ahead as Renfield and Berman, Jed and Elmer sat their mounts left of the trail, hidden in a clump of cottonwoods and stone-cold determined that, this time, they would achieve their purpose.

"This is how we're gonna do it," Jed mumbled through his bandana mask. "We hustle our critters onto the trail and get the drop on the crew, make the guard throw down his scattergun. Then, while you keep the crew covered, I'll warn the folks inside we'll shoot the crew 'less'n they foller orders."

"What's our first order gonna be?" Elmer wanted to know.

"Any man passengers armed, they gotta throw out their guns," declared Jed. "We ain't gonna have lead burnin' our asses this time, pal."

"They throw out their guns and — what comes next?" asked Elmer.

"We order the women out," decided Jed. "We dunno which one's the Dobson female, so we take no chances, get it done fast, make all of 'em hand over their gut-squeezers. I don't care how many of them contraptions we gotta tear apart. The map'll be in one of 'em."

"Okay, I got it," Elmer assured him. "So now we wait it out, huh?"

"Coach'll be along purty soon," Jed said confidently.

The stage passed the concealed Texans while they were spelling their animals.

"We ain't too far behind that rig," remarked Stretch.

"Nope," agreed Larry. "Couple more minutes and we'll be ready to move on, catch up with 'em easily."

Malone guided his team around a bend of the trail and onward toward the point marked by cottonwoods on their left. The northeastbound was making good time, he and his partner anticipating no trouble till they were nearing the trees.

Now the bandana masked horsemen emerged from the timber with pistols levelled, Jed bellowing a demand, and Britt cursed in frustration.

"Damn bastards got a clear bead on me, Harp!"

"Don't look like Hamill riders," frowned Malone, hauling back on his reins.

As the coach shuddered to a halt, the female passengers waxed apprehensive.

"Hold-up," scowled Dawson.

"Well now . . . " Pete said soothingly. "Let's all keep our heads, okay? No panic, ladies. Hundreds of travellers survive hold-ups."

"I guess we should — *try* to be calm," frowned Kitty.

"Disgraceful!" gasped Iris Dawson.

"Heaven help us!" cried Abigail.

"Amen," winced Eleanor.

Ordered to throw down his shotgun,

Joe Britt reluctantly did so. Malone growled at the bandits.

"We ain't carryin' gold nor cash, just passengers and mail."

"You hush your doggone mouth, driver!" snarled Jed. "All you gotta remember is my partner's trigger-finger's itchin' and he's aimin' at the guard's heart." He raised his voice to challenge the passengers. "Any man in there packin' a gun?"

Before Pete could answer, Dawson pantomimed for him to stay silent.

"Only one of us!" he called.

"Throw it out — or we blast the crew!" commanded Jed.

Against his better judgement, Pete again obeyed the older man's gesture. He unholstered his Colt and tossed it out the window.

"Just what d'you thievin' skunks want anyway?" Malone demanded.

"You'll find out," muttered Jed, walking his mount to the left side of the stalled vehicle. "How many women aboard?"

"Four," answered Dawson. "And what's it to you?"

"The women climb out and line up," ordered Jed. "The men stay inside."

"Now wait a minute . . . !" began Pete.

"They don't get hurt long as everybody follers orders," Jed said impatiently.

"Climb out — but don't be scared," Dawson softly urged the ladies. "I'm armed and, if he tries to lay a paw on any one of you, I'll yell 'drop' and, when you hit the ground, I'll put a bullet in him."

"C'mon!" Elmer yelled from up front. "We ain't got all day!"

"You're right," Britt whispered to Malone. "They *couldn't* be Hamill men."

Pete squeezed his wife's arm. She was first to alight, followed by the trembling Dudley sisters. Last to climb out, big Iris glowered at the horseman and pointed accusingly.

"I know you!" she boomed. "You're...!"

"No gabbin'!" commanded Jed. "Do

like I tell you and do it damn quick!"

"Get on with it!" urged Elmer.

"Now . . . !" Jed dilated his eyes threateningly. "Take them gowns off!"

"Do *what*?" gasped Kitty.

"Lord have mercy on us!" wailed Eleanor Dudley.

"Take off them gowns!" Jed repeated. "We want your corsets!"

"What the hell . . . ?" Malone began incredulously. "Joe, you hear what I heard?"

"I heard it, but I don't believe it," mumbled Britt.

"Shuddup!" chided Elmer.

"How *dare* you!" whooped Iris, quivering in indignation. "Such depravity! Outrageous! Despicable! Filthy degenerates!"

Incensed, she bent to pick up a rock. Dawson promptly drew his pistol and yelled.

"Drop!"

Confusion ensured. Kitty and the Dudley sisters went to ground, but the big woman was half-kneeling, grasping a fist-sized rock. Dawson thrust his gun out the leftside window and cut loose.

"Drat!" he chided himself. "Forgot my eyeglasses again!"

Shocked by the rock bouncing off his derby and the report from inside the coach, Jed fired and hit the corner of a trunk on the roof. Pete, who had noted where his Colt had fallen, threw himself out the open doorway to flop and shield his wife with his body, also the Dudley sisters if he could manage it. He could forget about reaching his six-gun.

Dawson's gun roared again — and again. He missed but, by how, the other hold-up man was one mighty startled desperado and Malone ready to take advantage of the distraction. The driver whipped out his Colt and cocked and fired too fast. At that, Elmer almost fainted; he felt the bullet's hot wind on his face, loosed a yell of fear and dug in his heels, wheeling his mount and hustling it to the cottonwoods. Jed too was discouraged. He fired into the coach and his slug sped through one window and embedded in the upholstery, missing Dawson by better than twenty-four inches. Then the bellowing Iris was hurling another rock. It bounced off the horse's rump and the animal reared, almost toppling Jed, who loosed an oath, regained control of the animal and turned to follow his accomplice.

The thwarted badmen charged through the cottonwoods and onward, making for thicker timber, better cover to the north, while Malone's Colt still boomed, Iris kept on hurling rocks and bellowing condemnation and Pete crawled to his fallen pistol, retrieved it and added its roar to the general din.

With the gunshots reaching them clearly, the Texans were on the move again, hustling their mounts onto the trail and kicking them to a gallop.

Up ahead, some distance from the scene of the hold-up, Renfield and Bermen were trading startled stares.

"Some helluva racket," growled Berman.

"What kind of a jinx is hounding us?" fumed Renfield. "All that shooting! It can only mean . . . !"

"Any fool could guess what it means," scowled Berman. "That damn stagecoach — somebody beat us to it. There's been a hold-up and the crew must've made a fight of it."

"Well, what the hell can we do?" wondered Renfield.

"Stay hidden and wait," decided Berman. "Better we don't show ourselves till we got some idea of what happened back there. A hold-up, sure, but did it backfire? We'll know soon enough — unless a team-horse stopped a bullet."

When the Texans came into view, their arrival heralded by the hoofbeats of the sorrel and pinto, Joe Britt had dropped from his perch and retrieved his shotgun. He had it cocked and aimed when Malone holstered his pistol and glanced backward.

151

"Hold your fire, Joe," he advised. "Just a couple cowhands. They heard shootin' and got curious."

Larry and Stretch reined up in a flurry of dust to be greeted by the Dobsons, who eagerly assured the crew and other passengers they had nothing to fear from the newcomers. The hold-up artists were a considerable distance away, they had disappeared into the tall timber due north, but were still in flight. The ladies had picked themselves up and were dusting themselves off, Iris Dawson still seething, the spinster sisters still trembling.

While Pete was speaking to the Texans, Malone and Britt traded knowing glances.

"Larry and Stretch, huh?" frowned the guard. "Well, if all we've heard of them is true . . ."

"Yeah," nodded Malone. "Raidin' stagecoaches ain't their style. Too bad they didn't get here sooner. Them sonsabitches'd be buzzard-bait now."

He climbed down and, with the

guard, joined the discussion.

"We were terrified!" blubbered Eleanor.

"Horrified!" cried Abigail.

"It was all — very frightening," sighed Kitty. "Driver, is there a medicine kit aboard? Some of the ladies would benefit from spirits of ammonia."

"Good slug of whiskey maybe," offered Stretch, delving into his saddlebag.

"I do not drink hard liquor," Iris said sternly.

"Yeah, well, *I'm* not temperance," said Dawson. "Thanks, friend, don't mind if I do."

"They weren't after the strongbox," Britt told the Texans.

"You ain't gonna believe what they were after," predicted Malone.

"Somethin' in the mail?" asked Larry.

"Somethin' on the females," retorted Malone.

"They were the same two fiends who broke into our room last night!" declared Iris.

"Same two, nothing surer," agreed her husband.

Having taken a stiff belt, he wiped the neck of the bottle and passed it to Pete, who shrugged, holstered his Colt and downed a reassuring mouthful.

"But, this time, my corset was not enough for them," Iris said indignantly. "They are subnormal blackguards with an unhealthy craving for ladies underwear."

"They ordered us — all four of us — to remove our outer clothing and surrender our corsets!" wailed Abigail.

"No two ways about it," Britt commented to Malone. "Could *never* be Hamill gunhawks. They only steal cash."

Larry remarked as discreetly as possible, out of deference to the ladies,

"It sure takes all kinds. My buddy and me, we've tangled with many a bandido, but never no girdle-grabbers."

"If this don't beat all," muttered an extremely puzzled Stretch. "I mean, bandidos just don't *do* that." And now he was stuck by a disturbing thought. "Anybody notice if — uh — one of 'em was kind of pear-shaped? Maybe that's it."

Larry was dubious.

"Wanted one of them things for *himself*?" he challenged.

"That sounds crazy," protested Kitty. "But if it's true, why would he steal *four* corsets?"

"So he'd be sure of gettin' one to fit?" Stretch lamely suggested.

"They are depraved, immoral misfits," insisted Iris. "That's the only explanation."

"They sure breedin' a strange kinda road agent nowadays, seems like," frowned Britt.

"Well, look now, we got a timetable," Malone pointed out. "Long as nobody suffered a hurt, we ought to get rollin' again." He eyed the Dudley sisters. "You ladies gonna faint or anything?"

"The danger has passed," sighed Abigail. "I think we feel better now."

"I'm so looking forward to resting

at Bald Rock Station," murmured Eleanor.

"If it'll make you folks feel any easier, we'll ride escort," offered Larry. "We got to bunk somewhere tonight and it might's well be a relay station."

"I know who you jaspers are, and I'd sure appreciate it," declared Malone.

The tall men unsheathed their Winchesters and nudged their mounts a few yards ahead of the team. Pete and Dawson helped the women reboard, climbed in after them and, the crew having taken their seats up top, the journey was resumed.

A short time later, hearing hoofbeats and the jingle of harness, Renfield and his companion hunched lower in their saddles and watched and waited.

"It wouldn't work," Berman muttered, when the vehicle and escorts appeared. "Not just the shotgun, but a couple rifles riding guard."

"There's a woman aboard that rig with a map to a fortune hidden in her damn underwear," scowled Renfield.

"She doesn't suspect it. Well, she couldn't be particularly smart, could she, marrying a loser like Dobson? But no doubt in my mind, Herb. You guessed right about what happened to the map."

"We can afford to be patient," said Berman, after the coach rolled by. "They're a long way from Scudder Creek, so time's working for us — there'll be other opportunities."

"We can't handle it alone," Renfield admitted.

"I think we're gonna have to deal Hamill in," said Berman. "I know the route to his hideaway. Starting from here, we could be talking turkey with him by noon tomorrow — so let's get started."

Being out of earshot of the passengers, the drifters didn't hesitate to discuss what they — what *anybody* — would have to regard as an unusual situation.

"Same two galoots," frowned Stretch. "And they ain't lettin' up. Hell's sakes, runt, how d'you figure a couple hombres that'd bust into a hotel room to lift a female's whatever you want to call it, skedaddle when the screamin' started, then try a stage hold-up for the same crazy reason?"

"I think you got it," Larry said scathingly. "Crazy you said. It's a loco reason for raidin' a stage, so they got to be squirrely, lamebrained, not a hundred cents to the dollar."

"All right then," agreed Stretch. "But they're dangerous to females just the same. It's some kind of itch and they can't lick it." He shook his head perplexedly. "And we thought we'd seen and heard everything."

"Any dumbhead that hankers for women's duds ain't worth frettin' about," shrugged Larry.

Gradually recovering their composure, the Dudley sisters wished Phineas Dawson would make no further mention of the hold-up. But big Iris's husband was still disgruntled.

"If I'd had my eye-glasses on I'd have seen clearer," he growled. "Could've

158

blown that bandit right off of his horse."

"Stop grouching, Phineas," chided Iris. "We all tend to be forgetful when we're excited." She folded her arms across her ample bosom and assured everybody, "At least we can be certain there'll be no repetition of such disgraceful attacks on our dignity, ladies. Twice those rogues have taken unpardonable liberties and twice they've been sent running."

"Right, Iris," Dawson nodded vehemently. "They wouldn't have the nerve to try it again, so there won't be a third time."

"I pray not," said Eleanor.

"You can depend on it, Miss Dudley," declared Dawson.

Pete took his wife's hand. She was staring out the window, her expression reflecting her unease.

"You all right, honey?" he asked softly. "Feeling easier now?"

"I'm no weakling," she shrugged. "You know it takes a lot to scare me."

"That's the truth," he nodded. "I didn't marry a chicken-hearted lady." He studied her, disturbed by her expression. "Something on your mind?"

"Yes," she said.

"Want to talk about it?" he offered.

"Not here and now," she said. "Let's wait till we reach the relay station. I'd as soon we speak of it in private."

"Not fretting about this, are you?" he challenged, indicating the dressing on his face. "It doesn't hurt at all. I could pull this thing off right now."

"No, we'll wait till tomorrow morning," she said. "I'll take if off and put on a fresh dressing just as the Bellamy doctor said I should."

"You're the boss," he shrugged.

"No I'm not — you are," she retorted affectionately. "You're the boss of P-Bar-D and my husband. I'm the lady of the house." He still held her hand. She was silent a long moment. Then, "It's comforting, isn't it, just knowing they're near?"

"Larry and Stretch?" he grinned. "Uh huh. Something about them. They're so all-fired casual, but you always have the feeling they can handle any trouble, anything at all."

"That's what I mean," she nodded. "As for you, Pete dear, you can be quick-thinking and protective when needed. I'm not forgetting how you leapt out of this coach and tried to shield not just me but others too."

Around sundown, when the stage reached the relay station, passengers and crew won a genial welcome from the two families in charge of this outpost. The house was double-storied and stoutly constructed, all its rooms austerely but comfortably furnished. At Bald Rock, accommodation was no problem; the Texans were offered their choice of a two-bed room or a couple of singles.

The travellers availed themselves of the bathing facilities before assembling in the big dining room for a substantial supper. Tables for four had been laid. Something about Kitty Dobson's demeanor warned Larry she wanted to be alone with her husband, so he and Stretch shared a table with the crew and some friendly conversation with their meal.

"Is this private enough?" Pete asked. "I don't think we could be overheard if you keep your voice down."

"Very well," Kitty said half-way through the first course. "I'll tell you what's troubling me, and you'll wonder why it didn't occur to me last night in Bellamy."

"Okay," he nodded. "I'm listening."

"What did I inherit from Aunt Elly?" she softly challenged. "And what are those bandits trying to steal?"

"Hol-eee Moses!" frowned Pete Dobson.

# 6

## Far From Home And Vulnerable

STRETCH, during a lull in the suppertime conversation, glanced to the corner table shared by the young couple and remarked to his partner,

"The young folks look a mite spooked."

"Sure do," noted Larry. "Well, you can't blame 'em."

"Me and Joe're used to it," Malone mumbled while munching. "But ordinary folks, travellers, it's rougher on them."

"Plays hell with their nerves, a hold-up," nodded Britt. "Specially the women. Couple gunshots'll scare 'em bad every time." He added, to Larry's amusement, "Women oughtn't travel anyway, ought to just stay where they're at."

163

Pete was eyeing his wife incredulously.

"Well, there must be *some* reason," she insisted.

"Why would any thief want what Aunt Ellie left you?" he wondered. "No, it makes no sense. You're forgetting something. It wasn't our room they broke into and, when they stopped the stage, they didn't call just you out. They wanted — uh — whatever the other women're wearing under their gowns."

"Yes, that's how it was," she frowned. "So I suppose it's just coincidence."

"Doesn't it strike you Mrs Dawson could be right?" He was able to grin again, reassuring her. "They're tetched." He raised finger to temple. "A couple of real strange characters. What would they do with a corset they took a liking to? Probably what Hardrock Skimmer did. Keep it for a good luck piece."

"Hardrock Skimmer?"

"Crazy old fossicker my pa told me of, but not till after my voice broke. In the old days, right after the Comstock Lode was discovered, mining camps sprung up all over California. There were always cheap saloons, bordellos, dance halls and such . . . "

"I can imagine."

"And girls. You know the kind."

"Not personally — and I hope my husband doesn't."

"Heck, no. But you know what I mean. Satin gowns and gaudy do-dads. Anyway, there was one girl Hardrock must've got hot about, so what do you suppose he did? Busted into her room. No, he didn't even touch her. He was fast asleep and he only stole one thing, one of her fancy garters. And that was his good luck piece. Poor old feller never made a lucky strike but, everywhere he went, he kept that darn garter, figuring it'd change his luck. Pa said, when Hardrock died, they probably buried it with him."

"So," mused Kitty. "Those foolish robbers . . . "

"Foolish is how they look, that's for

sure," chuckled Pete. "One of 'em fat, one of 'em skinny, the dented derbies and, when they get to shooting, they aren't exactly the surest shots in the whole state of Nevada. No, honey, I don't believe any thief craves to make off with your purty new corset."

"You're probably right," she agreed, or seemed to.

"So you can stop worrying," he said encouragingly.

"Yes, very well," said Kitty. "I'll stop worrying."

But she didn't sleep well that night.

As for Jed and Elmer, there was to be precious little sleep for them. After two abortive attempts, Jed was now obsessed. Come what may, the corset containing the map to the Sierra Stash would be his and Elmer's to share.

"Ain't gonna let nothin' stop me," he vowed, when they at last made camp to cook a meal. "Not bullets, not that guard's scattergun, not nothin'!"

His fever was perhaps contagious. Elmer, though shuddering from memories of big Iris's fearsome indignation, was now as committed as his partner. And, for once, using his brain, pondering, thinking clearly.

"Orderin' all them women outa the coach was our big mistake," he muttered. "Only one of 'em's wearin' that thing. Mightn't of been such a goshawful ruckus if we'd just hollered for the Dobson woman."

"That's what I'm gonna do next time," Jed assured him. "And we're gonna make damn sure the coach stops where we want it to."

Jed's plan was to block the trail somewhere beyond a night stop of the northeastbound. Felling a tree was what he had in mind and, for this, they would require an axe. No problem. In the dead of night, they purloined that essential item from an outlying homestead. It was right there, its head embedded in a stump serving as a chopping block; they only had to yank it free and continue on their way.

After Bald Rock, the next noon stop

along this Wells Fargo route was the sleepy settlement of Quinoza, just lunch and a team-switch, then on to their next overnight stop, Tealsburg, the destination of the Dudley sisters. To the gratitude of the female passengers and approval of the crew, the Texans kept tagging the coach, riding clear of the trail, but keeping the vehicle in sight.

In the hour before noon, with Berman his guide, Clove Renfield reached the hideout of the infamous Hamill gang. The camp was located atop a woody mesa in high country, surrounded by terrain devoid of cover; no posse could approach undetected and, from their vantage-point, Hamill riflemen could wreak havoc on advancing riders.

But no shots were triggered as these riders made for the north slope.

"Lookout with a spyglass," Berman assured Renfield. "He recognized me. None of the old bunch would forget my face, so you can stop worrying. We won't be shot at."

The lookout watched the horsemen begin the ascent. He was a lean character, lank-haired with a pointed chin, his weapons a tied-down .45 and a Winchester. Lowering the telescope, Slim Raitt turned and called to the three shabbily-garbed men squatting by the fire on which their midday meal cooked. For shelter, the four survivors of the once seven-strong band were using a tent and two bark and tarpaper lean-tos. A rough corral of trimmed branches housed their horses.

"Company you say?" Reno Hamill rose to his feet. He was a shade under six feet tall and so blond as to be almost albino, his pale brows and mustache matching the hair straggling from under a black Stetson. The eyes were pale blue, the nose sharp, the mouth thin-lipped. "You don't look spooked — so it's somebody we know?"

"One of 'em's familiar, but I can't recall where I saw his kisser before," said Raitt. "The other's Herb."

"Herb Berman?" Hamill chuckled softly. "Well, well, well. All the way from California comes our old companero."

One of the still seated men, barrel-chested Johnny Deuce, drew a sleeve across his mouth and grinned sardonically.

"Might be Herb dropped his last dollar playin' blackjack or faro," he remarked. "If he's come back to beg for a handout, that'll be a real laugh, the shape we're in."

"I dunno if Herb'd have the nerve," drawled the fourth man, the brawny, broken-nosed Tully Williams. "He was so damn sure he'd clean up when he quit the outfit and headed west."

"He's an old friend," shrugged Hamill. "I wouldn't have let him go if I couldn't trust him. No chance he'd tip the law where we're holed up. Johnny, maybe they'll be hungry. Throw some more beans in the pan and get some more coffee goin'."

The outlaws waited some little time.

Climbing the slope was hard on horses, an ascent that couldn't be rushed. When Renfield and Berman finally appeared, their animals were panting.

"Good to see you, Reno," grinned Berman.

"Same here," nodded Hamill. "Who's your friend that Slim's tryin' to remember?"

"The name's Clive Renfield," Berman offered as they reined up. "You're gonna be interested, Reno. The name Marchmount mean anything to you? He's kin to the Marchmounts."

"Wouldn't be many ain't heard *that* name," frowned Johnny Deuce. "Old Clute, first of the line, and his Sierra Stash."

The horses were offsaddled and tended by Williams. By the time the newcomers were settling down to satisfy their appetites, Renfield had been introduced to Hamill and the other men and Deuce was fetching a newspaper from the tent.

"Him for sure," he told the

boss-bandit. "He's kin all right. Nephew to the old man."

"Big news travels far and fast," remarked Berman. "And Ellie March-mount's death could never be a secret, her being old Clute's widow."

"Does that paper report the reading of the will, the disposal of the estate?" asked Renfield. Deuce nodded, studying him with keen interest. "So you all know how I came out of it. Just the old man's clothes, nothing else."

"And Clive searched every garment carefully," Berman assured Hamill. "You can guess why, huh?"

"I can guess," said Hamill, eyeing Renfield. "No luck? It wasn't hid in the old jasper's duds, stowed away in a boot maybe, sweatband of a hat? I bet you searched *real* careful, and we know for what, don't we?"

"I'm sure we have the same idea," said Renfield.

"Nobody that ever heard of March-mount's cache is gonna believe there ain't no map," muttered Hamill.

"But, like it says in the paper, no kin of the old gal got it," said Deuce.

"And that don't add up right," complained Raitt, who was eating, but moving back and forth, still checking to assure himself the new arrivals had not been followed. "She wouldn't have burned it. Nobody but a damn lunatic'd burn the map to the Sierra Stash."

"Right," agreed Renfield. "And you can take it from me, because I visited her all the time, including during her last illness. My aunt was kind of whimsical, a joker just like old Clute himself, but not eccentric, nothing wrong with her thinking. She was never feeble-minded."

"All right," prodded Hamill. "You gettin' around to makin' a point?"

"I talked it over with Herb," said Renfield. "He came up with an idea and, to me, it makes sense·— *has* to be the answer. Ready to tell 'em about it, Herb?"

"This'll mean a six-way share-out," Berman reminded him.

173

"Fine by me," said Renfield.

"Which reminds me," frowned Berman, glancing around. "How about the rest of the old gang, Reno? When I pulled out, there were six of you left. I don't see Caddow or McNear."

"This is all of us," said Hamill. "When we took the Settlers' Bank at San Luiz, some citizen got Caddow with a lucky shot."

"Right 'tween his eyes," Williams mumbled with his mouth full.

"And McNear, he was gettin' old," shrugged Hamill. "Chill got his lungs last winter. Pneumonia I guess. His grave's over Cannon Ridge way. No marker. No scavenger's ever gonna find his carcass."

"But don't sell us short, Herb," muttered Deuce. "The four of us'll score again next time Reno sets up a deal."

"The next deal could be your last," Berman told his old leader. "I've figured where the map is. When we get it, we'll find the Marchmount cache and there'll be gold enough for all of us. For the rest of our lives, we'll be living high off the hog. We could all head east and no lawman would ever hear of the Hamill gang again."

"How strong's your hunch?" challenged Hamill.

"Reno, I've pondered on it, figured it from every angle, and I *have* to be right," declared Berman. "I'll explain everything and . . . "

"And there'll be a lot of laughing here," Renfield predicted. "It'll sound comical, so you'll all laugh." He added firmly, "But then, when you think it over, you'll see the logic of it. Go on, Herb. One point at a time."

Berman talked for some ten minutes, stressing significant aspects of the situation, the fact that Kitty Dobson had won her aged aunt's deep affection and admiration and had herself expected to collect a generous inheritance. When he spoke of Kitty's bequest, the reaction was as Renfield anticipated, raucous laughter, an obscene comment or two.

Hamill joined in but, impressed by Berman's patience, ordered his men to silence.

"I never heard Herb talk foolish," he muttered. "So let him finish."

"Just a damn corset," said Berman. "Funny? Sure, it's funny. But, of all of them, including her sons and their wives, the Dobson woman was the only one the old girl doted on." He nodded to Renfield. "Go on. Convince them."

"It's the truth," growled Renfield. "Every time we talked it was the same damn thing, her grouching at me, complaining of my gambling, describing Brad and Sam as a couple of stuff-shirts and their wives as vain and unfeeling. Kitty Dobson was the only one she had a good word for — a lot of good words. Kitty had a brain in her head and a kind heart. Kitty was genuine. Kitty married a good man. Kitty respected her. Kitty was this and that, all of it in her favor. So it's a hundred percent reasonable.

That piece of underwear is camouflage for the map. Old Ellie counted on Kitty finding it sooner or later — and we'd better hope it's not sooner."

Hamill broke the pensive silence following Renfield's declaration.

"I ain't laughin' any more," he announced. "I'm buyin' Herb's hunch. How about you, Johnny — Slim — Tully . . . ?"

"It's loco," was Deuce's comment. "Loco enough to be true."

Raitt and Williams nodded agreement, and Renfield was profoundly impressed by Hamill's next move. The boss-bandit snapped his fingers and voiced a command. Williams drained his tin cup, rose and hurried to the tent.

"A timetable?" frowned Renfield. "Hamill, my hat's off to you."

"Wells Fargo schedule," grinned Hamill. "In my business, I need to know all the routes and where a coach'll be at any time. Northeast for Scudder Creek, huh? Well now, them Dobsons are far from home."

"And vulnerable," enthused Berman.

"Let's see now," drawled Hamill, when Williams returned with the time-table. "Boarded the last northeastbound at Bellamy you said. Means they're noonin' at Quinoza right now and they'll overnight at Tealsburg. We'll be movin' out when we're through eatin', but we couldn't make the trail beyond Tealsburg in time to set up an ambush. Better we ride all the short-cuts, head for another overnight stop, Arnold City. We can do that without killin' our horses."

"Like old times, Reno," chuckled Berman. "We'll be six."

"And six is plenty," nodded Hamill. "We'll get what we're after and we'll get out alive. As for the crew and any traveller tries gettin' 'tween us and the woman . . . " He shrugged callously, "maybe we'll have to gun 'em down. But what the hell? They won't be our first kills."

By 1.15 p.m. the six-strong rogue pack was on the move, quitting the

178

Hamill lair, the hideout to which they would never return.

* * *

Lunch at Quinoza had been a somewhat indigestible meal, but only the Dawsons were complaining when the stage resumed its run. The Dudley sisters were in good humor, looking forward to sighting their hometown by sundown. And the Dobsons were quiet, Pete concerned that his wife was obviously preoccupied and, he suspected, apprehensive.

He refrained from comment till the Dawsons were dozing and the sisters engrossed in their own conversation.

"You keep looking out the window and ahead," he said quietly. "Don't worry. Larry and Stretch aren't too far off. You mightn't see 'em, but they're around."

She withdrew her head and, with her face close to his, murmured,

"I want to talk to them, Pete. Tonight

179

would be best. We could ask them to our room."

"You're still fretting," he accused.

"I've tried, but it stays in my mind," she complained. "It has to mean something, those bandits so — well — they seemed frantic to me. Why would bandits demand what they demanded — instead of money?"

"Couldn't be any connection . . . " he began.

"We've talked about it, you've tried to sooth me, but I still have this uneasy feeling," she said. "We trust them, don't we? And Larry has a reputation for, you know, solving all kinds of problems."

"He sure has," he agreed. "All right, if that's what you want, why not?"

No delays, no incidents between Quinoza and Tealsburg. At the Wells Fargo depot there, the sisters farewelled their fellow travellers and went their way. Overnight passengers were accommodated at the Wyman House, a middle-class hotel at which the Texans were able to rent a couple of singles.

It was while the tall men were at supper with the other guests that Pete came to them and made his request.

"Why, sure," nodded Stretch. "We'll be glad to look in on you."

"Somethin' botherin' you, Pete?" asked Larry.

"Kitty more than me," confided Pete. "Says she'll be easier in her mind if you'll listen to what's fazing her."

"Well," shrugged Larry. "I'm a good listener."

"Right after supper?" begged Pete. "We're in Room 5 upstairs."

"When you're through eatin', we'll follow you up," promised Larry.

When the young rancher rejoined his wife, Stretch winced.

"Here we go again," he muttered.

"Meanin'?" prodded Larry.

"Meanin' the same old thing," grouched Stretch. "Somebody's frettin' about somethin', they lay it on us and, next thing we know, we're buyin' trouble again."

"You worry too much," chided Larry.

"No, I don't worry at all," countered Stretch. "You do all the worryin'. And I just tag along."

After supper, they joined the Dobsons in Room 5. Pete fished out his makings and, after urging the tall men to do likewise, Kitty began confiding in them. They built and lit cigarettes and gave her their undivided attention.

"I'm not going to blush and hold anything back," she said bluntly. "I know you're bachelors, but I'm sure you aren't ignorant about — well, darn it, you know women wear corsets."

Stretch didn't know which way to look. Not so Larry. He eyed both Dobsons steadily and remarked,

"Been a lot of talk of such contraptions lately."

"And peculiar things keep happening," mused Pete. "First a couple hombres try to make off with Ma Dawson's corset at the Bellamy hotel, then the same two galoots hold up the stage and order — I couldn't believe 'em when I heard it — order every woman on the coach to hand over her dog-gone corset."

"You got the right word for it, Pete," nodded Larry. "Peculiar." Then he eyed Kitty again. "You got somethin' else to say, right?"

"I was bashful about it first time we talked," she said. "But I don't have to be, do I? You're our friends now, so it won't embarrass me to tell you. It's about — what I inherited from Aunt Ellie Marchmount in Sacramento."

She paced and talked with the guests hanging on her every word. They readily appreciated her surprise and disappointment when the bequest was announced and agreed it was reasonable that she had anticipated a sum of cash, if only a similar amount to that bequeathed to the servants.

Pete now threw in a remark the significance of which intrigued Larry.

"After all, the old lady liked Kitty best."

"Howzat again?" frowned Larry.

"I mean — more than the others," said Pete. "Even Brad and Sam and their wives."

"You were her favourite, kind of?" Larry asked Kitty.

"She always said so in her letters," nodded Kitty.

"Well now, pardon me for askin' on account of this is personal." Larry ran a pensive eye over her, then concentrated on her trim waist. "You're wearin' it now?"

"I've worn it since I got it," she said. Then she hesitated. "Oh, what does it matter? I promised myself I wouldn't be embarrassed, so why shouldn't you know? My old one was all worn out, so I was only too grateful for the new one."

"You had a chance to — kind of study it?" Larry persisted. "Anything special about it, anything different? Maybe it's got beads on it that ain't just beads — might be genuine jewels." She shook her head. "No? So now you're wonderin' about them dumb thieves, thinkin' maybe that's what they're after. Not Mrs Dawsons, but yours."

"I did have that thought," said Kitty. "But why do they want it so badly? It's fine quality, the best I've ever had, but just a corset after all."

"Somebody knows something you don't know, honey." Pete waxed facetious and grinned at Stretch. "Maybe Aunt Ellie sewed a lot of hundred dollar bills into it."

Stretch returned his grin. Kitty grimaced impatiently. Larry neither grinned nor grimaced. It was a jocular remark, but . . .

"Why couldn't that be so?" he frowned. "Was your aunt handy with needle and thread?"

"Did beautiful needlework," said Kitty.

"I was joking," protested Pete.

"Sure, but you could be right," suggested Larry. "Anyway, Kitty ought to check. Tell you what. My partner and me, we'll wait outside. Call us in when — uh — it's okay for us to look at it."

"I'll come with you," decided Pete. "She can get out of that thing by herself, doesn't need my help."

"I'll need only a few minutes," Kitty assured them as they filed out.

Pete closed the door, traded stares with the Texans and wondered,

"Did I say something dumb that could turn out to be something smart?"

"Anything's possible, amigo," shrugged Larry. "There's just one angle I can't savvy. The old lady was powerful fond of your wife, yet all she left her was that contraption. Think about it. Does it sound reasonable to you?"

"No, it doesn't," Pete admitted.

A few moments later, responding to Kitty's summons, they rejoined her. She had finished refastening her gown and, at first, Larry ignored the item now spread on the table. He supposed it wasn't for him to ponder such inconsistencies but, to his bachelor eye, it didn't appear Kitty Dobson needed a corset; she appeared as trim-figured without it.

"I felt at it," she told them.

"Feel anything that could be paper cash — greenbacks?" asked her husband.

"I don't know if it's cash," she said. "Whatever it is, it's only in one place. I felt all around it, but there's just this . . . " She beckoned the tall men. "Come feel it for yourselves."

"Uh — I couldn't . . . " mumbled Stretch, averting his eyes.

"Look at Stretch," she giggled. "He's too sheepish to . . . "

"I ain't," said Larry, stepping forward. "Point to which part."

"This part."

She placed a finger on it. He felt at it with all his fingers, his thumb also. For good measure, he examined the whole foundation garment.

"*Somethin*' there," he muttered. "Flat, so you wouldn't notice if you weren't feelin' for it. So what d'you say, Kitty? You curious enough to . . . ?"

He produced his jack-knife. Horrified, she raised a hand.

"Not with *that*. This is a woman's chore, and I'll use my scissors. If I snip the stitching carefully, there'll be no real damage. I'll be able to restitch it and the corset'll be good as new."

The men reseated themselves, smoking, waiting patiently; no point in hustling her. As she went to work, she remarked on the quality of the material and opined this was her late aunt's needle-work. Better than ten minutes passed, and then she had cut sufficient stitching to make a four-inch opening into which she could insert finger and thumb.

"Something there?" demanded Pete.

"Yes, and it's sliding out easily," she replied. "It's flat and it feels smooth and — why — it's folded oilskin."

Discarding the corset, she placed the small package on the table — and hesitated.

"What're you waiting for, sweetheart?" Pete nodded encouragingly. "Whatever it is, it's yours, part of your inheritance."

"I — guess so," she said warily.

The men hovered around her, watching as she unwrapped the oilskin. All the package contained was a folded square of yellowing paper.

"Careful, take your time," frowned Pete. "Don't tear it."

The paper, when unfolded, was six inches wide and eight inches long. The ink had faded, but the lines and marks and inscriptions were still discernible. The Dobsons gawked at each other. Stretch loosed a low whistle and Larry said emphatically.

"Jackpot. Look at them signs, the arrow and all. What you got here is old Clute's handiwork, his map to what they call the Sierra Stash, his cached nuggets. See? There's his name printed in the bottom right corner."

"Oh, Lord!" breathed Kitty.

"Holy Moses!" gasped her husband. "Your aunt was more generous than you hoped!"

"Somebody else knows," warned Larry. "They know — or they guessed.

Don't matter which. No mystery any more. This is what they wanted, the galoots that busted into the wrong room at Givney's and held up the stage."

Pete, rallying from his initial shock, said grimly,

"And we're still a long way from Scudder Creek."

"Runt, this'd be a real fine time for you to come up with an idea," urged Stretch. "Get your brains workin', *think* of somethin' like you always do."

"One thing about the break-in I didn't take kindly to," muttered Larry. "The hold-up too. There was gunplay. Dawson or his wife could've stopped a bullet. Any lady on the coach could've got hurt or killed, them or the crew. I don't want that to happen again — and it needn't — because there's an easy way of shakin' them fool road agents off our backs."

"Well, fine," said Pete. "Anything we can do to help?"

"Kitty'll have to do most of it," said Larry, matching stares with her.

"You got plenty thread?" She nodded. "That's mightly fortunate because, as well as stitchin' what you just cut, you'll be doin' some more sewin' before you turn in." He nodded to the corset. "Them things come in sizes like a man's duds?" Another nod. "Mind tellin' me your size?" After she answered, he fished out his wallet and turned to his partner.

"Think you can remember them numbers?"

Sure," shrugged Stretch. "Easy."

"Bueno." Larry pressed a few bills into his hand. "Stores stay open later when travellers overnight in a town along the stage route. Get goin', beanpole. Find a ladies store, buy a corset and fetch it back here pronto."

"I'm on my way," Stretch said promptly, after which he hurried out.

"He'll be back in a minute," Larry predicted to the Dobsons. "Maybe a few seconds."

The taller Texan had retrieved his hat from his room and was headed for the stairs before the full significance of Larry's command hit him like a physical blow. The door to the Dobsons's room opened again. He loomed on the threshold, staring aghast at Larry.

"You want me — to do *what* . . . ?"

"You heard, so don't linger," ordered Larry. "Sooner you get back, sooner Kitty can get started."

"*Me?*" Stretch was shocked to the core, dismayed, sweating. "I got to — go and — buy . . . ?"

"Plain enough, ain't it?" challenged Larry. "Hustle!"

"I ain't never gonna forgive you for this," declared the taller Texan.

"Well," said Larry. "That's a chance I just have to take."

Stretch departed. Larry now instructed Kitty and her husband to choose a safe hiding place for the map, but not rightaway. It was something for them to decide between themselves. Meanwhile, he would need pen, ink and paper. Pete was urged to fetch these articles and warned the paper should be plain, just one sheet not bearing the emblem of the hotel; maybe the night-clerk would oblige. Pete eyed him dubiously as he started for the door.

"You mean to make a copy of the map?"

"*That'll* be the day," Larry growled with a mirthless grin. "Go on, Pete. There's gonna be a map for them dumb bandidos sure enough, but it'll lead 'em a long ways from where old Clute stashed his gold."

Left alone with Kitty, he became conscious of her intent appraisal. And she was smiling.

"Larry Valentine, you have a mean mind and you're just full of dirty tricks," she declared. "And how I admire you for your — your cunning and your shifty notions."

It was meant as a compliment. Realizing this, he grinned at her.

"You guessed, huh?"

"I've guessed, she nodded. "And I just *love* it!"

Stretch, meanwhile, was walking

193

Tealsburg's main street in acute misery and being sized up by the tobacco-chewing, scrawny Jethro Ackers, deputy to the town marshal. Initially, Ackers was merely intrigued by the stranger's generous height. But then the tall man entered the store of Miss Hedda Hayes, who specialized in ribbons and laces and other fripperies so vital to the opposite sex, including undergarments. Really curious now, the deputy crossed the street to prop a shoulder in the entrance to Miss Hayes's establishment.

A small, elderly lady smiled at Stretch from behind the counter, and his ordeal began.

# 7

## Girdle Of Deception

"**D**EARY deary me, such a tall gentleman," exclaimed Miss Hayes. "And wearing two pistols. Heavens to Betsy, if you mean to rob me . . . "

"Now, ma'am . . . " began Stretch, doffing his Stetson.

"He ain't gonna rob you, Miss Hedda," Ackers drawled from the doorway. "Not right before the eyes of the law."

Stretch threw a glance over his shoulder, winced and returned his gaze to the small woman.

"I ain't no thief," he assured her. "Gotta buy somethin', ma'am, and here's the cash."

As a gesture of peaceful intentions, he fished out the banknotes given him by his partner and placed them on the counter.

"Well, certainly, sir," she beamed. "And what is it you wish, pray?"

Stretch cleared his throat, bowed his head and mumbled his requirement and the size thereof. She didn't raise her eyebrows. But Ackers raised his. He also frowned and stroked his chin.

"You got one that size, ma'am?" asked Stretch.

"Of course," she nodded. "It's a common size. And the color? I can let you have pink . . . "

"It oughtn't be pink," frowned Stretch.

"Nope," grunted Ackers, shifting his chaw to the other side of his mouth. "Oughtn't be pink."

Though glaring at him, Stretch refrained from cussing out of deference to the little lady whose help he so desperately needed.

"You got white?" he enquired.

"White, by all means." Miss Hayes was lost from view under the counter for a few moments. Stretch looked to the doorway again. The deputy was still there, shoulder propped, jaws chomping, face impassive. "Here we are." Miss Hayes rose and displayed the corset for his inspection. "Very popular, I assure you. My regular customers favor this style."

"Looks good to me," commented Ackers.

"That'll do fine, ma'am." Stretch said hastily. "How much?"

She took only one of the banknotes and gave him change. He gathered up the money and pocketed it.

"Won't take me a moment to wrap it," said Miss Hayes.

"I'm sure beholden, ma'am," he mumbled.

"Men," she mused while making the parcel. "I declare they fuss so. Now, when I stop by Mister Brohaldt's store to buy underwear for my dear brother, I'm not in the least embarrassed. But men! Really, sir, you should be proud. I'm sure your wife will be very satisfied."

"Ain't got no wife," said Stretch.

"Oh," said Miss Hayes.

She proffered the parcel. He tucked it under an arm, thanked her politely and turned to leave. The way he felt at this time, it was fortunate the deputy wasn't blocking the doorway; he would have belted him all the way into the street. Ackers stood aside, but followed him a few paces.

"I don't savvy," he mumbled around his chaw.

"I'll bet you don't," growled Stretch, still walking.

"You don't *need* it, mister," Ackers insisted.

"Ain't for me," Stretch said through clenched teeth.

"No?" prodded Ackers.

"It's for my horse," said Stretch. "He's gettin' fat, and he's plumb embarrassed about it."

The deputy guffawed, slapped his knee, then made a frantic gasping sound and pressed hand to belly.

"Damn! You made me swaller my chaw!"

"I'm sorry," sneered Stretch. "Sorry you didn't choke on it."

When he re-entered the Dobson room a few minutes later, his partner was seated at the table, busy with pen and ink. Without looking up, Larry said,

"Give it to Kitty. She knows what she has to do."

"That was the worst thing I ever had to do in my whole doggone life!" fumed Stretch, while the Dobsons traded smiles. "I ain't never been so humiliated!"

"You got what we need," muttered Larry. "You did somethin' mighty important. I had to trust you to do it right, and you never let me down."

"Don't try honey-talkin' me, runt," scowled Stretch. He stood by Larry's chair after surrendering the parcel to Kitty. "What're you doin?"

"Fixin' to make a couple lame brained thieves happy," said Larry.

He paused to show Kitty an approving grin. "Smart notion you had. I said the ink has to look faded and you just mixed a little water in it." He resumed his chore. "Pete, you didn't marry no slow-witted lady."

"I know it," grinned Pete.

A few more strokes and notations and the substitute map was finished — on a clean sheet of paper contrasting sharply with Clute Marchmount's original. The substitute was subjected to a makeshift ageing process, first crumpled, then rubbed against the sole of Larry's boot. The window-sill needed dusting; smoothed out, the paper was smeared along it. Pete got into the spirit of the thing, investigated the back of a Currier & Ives print hung on the south wall. It too had gathered dust. He dampered a kerchief, collected grime and, while Larry held the paper steady, both sides were smeared. The sheet was crumpled again, then smoothed out and folded to match the creases in the square of oilskin.

"How you hide the real map's your business," Larry told the young couple. "Kitty, you know what to do with this fake."

"I know exactly what to do," she nodded.

The fake was tightly folded into the oilskin. It was now a facsimile of the wad secreted in Kitty's gift from her aunt. She seated herself, spread the item purchased by Stretch on her lap and got to work with the point of her scissors. And, as she snipped, Stretch caught on.

"Now I savvy your dirty trick," he growled at his partner. "But I'm still mad at you."

"I can think of a couple jackasses that'll end up a whole lot madder," countered Larry, and Pete began chuckling. He rolled and lit a cigarette, nodded to Stretch and rose to leave, his eyes on Kitty again. "So, if you run into another ambush, you know what you got to do?"

"I understand," she assured him.

"Depend on me, Larry I'll make it convincing."

Kitty's chore ended around 10.15. The Dobsons, the Dawsons and the Texans enjoyed uninterrupted sleep this night and, after breakfast at the hotel, walked to the depot where they met a passenger boarding here. Beasley was the name, booze his game; he was a liquor drummer, dapper, scrupulously courteous to Kitty and big Iris.

The Texans, who had fetched their saddled horses, had a few words with the stage crew before mounting and moving out.

"We'll be ahead, alongside of you or followin' close," Larry assured them. "Stay loose now. If them road agents show 'emselves again, whip up the team and keep goin'. We got somethin' planned, so you can bet they won't try chasin' you."

"All right," said Malone. "We switch teams and eat at the noon stop, Cafferty's Well, and overnight in Masonville, okay?"

"We'll be seein' you," promised Larry.

The run from Tealsburg to the relay station was incident-free because, by 10.45 that morning, Jed and Elmer had chosen their new ambush site which was half-way between Cafferty's Well and the night stop.

Hard at work they were, taking turns to use their purloined axe, attacking a tall tree soaring beside the trail. The strategy was simple and therefore appropriate to their mentality. However, it would require perfect timing, and when had their timing ever been perfect?

"We — can't — miss . . ." panted Jed, swinging, sending chips flying while his sidekick squatted exhausted. "We topple it so it falls across the trail — blocks 'em. And that'll be — such a shock — the guard won't even get his scattergun cocked. Then we — holler for the Dobson woman — to hand over that dang-blasted corset."

It was 2.15 p.m. when they heard

the coach coming, at which time the Texans were studying the scene from behind the rocks atop a low ridge left of the trail. Taking his turn with the axe, Elmer gasped and wheezed and hacked frantically, to the grim amusement of the man surveying him through field-glasses.

"Pitiful," Larry remarked, passing the binoculars to his partner.

Stretch took a look, sighed heavily and returned the glasses.

"Ain't that the truth," he agreed. "Plumb pitiful."

"I could feel sorry for 'em," declared Larry, "if they weren't a couple no-good thieves. Well, they're about to get what they want — they think."

The coach approached at brisk speed and, in anguish, Jed drew his six-gun.

"No use!" he cried. "We'll never cut'er through in time! Forget the axe! Draw your hogleg, pal!"

Pete thrust his head out to scan the ridge, sighted the Texans and caught Larry's signal.

"This is it, honey," he muttered. "Get set."

The whiskey drummer's eyes popped. The Dawsons blinked incredulously as Kitty unwrapped the parcel in her lap and edged to the rightside window. Onto the trail directly ahead stumbled the bone-weary robbers, brandishing their pistols, yelling. Joe Britt growled ferociously and cocked his shotgun. Malone urged his team to a hard run and the robbers had two choices — stand their ground and be run down or jump clear.

They jumped, and then Kitty screamed at them and hurled the corset out.

"Take it! This is what you want! Take it — and stop hounding us!"

To the wonderment of Jed and Elmer, the foundation garment flew through the air to fall a few yards from where they had flopped. They lurched upright and the stage sped on and the tall riders promptly lost interest in the road agents and continued on toward the ridge's far end. After an exchange of startled glances, Jed and Elmer stumbled to the surrendered item.

Jed gathered it up and loosed a whoop.

"We got it!"

"Hot damn!" enthused Elmer. "We spooked her. She couldn't take any more of our deviltry."

"All ours," gloated Jed. "Looky here. You can see where somethin's sewed into it. We've scored, Elmer — at last!" He froze, held the corset to his chest and flinched apprehensively. "What's that?"

"What's what?" asked Elmer.

"A groanin', cracklin' sound," frowned Jed.

Elmer flicked an uneasy glance to his right.

"Jumpin' Jericho! Damn tree's a'comin' down!"

They scuttled as far clear as their aching legs could carry them and, predictably, in the wrong direction. Even so, they were lucky. The tree crashed across the trail but level with it, only the topmost foliage pinning them.

After extricating themselves, they scampered to their ground-reined horses, swung astride and took off, headed nowhere in particular until they sighted a stand of timber.

"In there!" yelled Jed. "Foller me!"

"Foller you?" gasped Elmer. "Where the hell else'd I go? You got the belly-squeezer — with Marchmount's map in it."

Inside the timber, they found a clearing. Dismounting, they again ground-reined their animals, after which Jed bared his teeth and drew a knife. Elmer pleaded with him to take care. Slashed in several places, the map could be useless to them. Jed hunkered and began attacking Kitty Dobson's stitching with the point of his blade. Then he lost patience, grasped the outer material and ripped it and the flat package slid to the ground.

He unwrapped the oilskin, then the paper, which he unfolded with his fingers shaking. Elmer took one look, tried to whistle, failed and flopped on his backside.

"Bonanza!" he breathed.

"This is *it*!" leered Jed. "Look at it. Old Clute drawed it better'n twenty years ago, but we can still read it, still makes sense of it. See? Here where it says 'Dig here'? That's where it's at — Marchmount's pile — the Sierra Stash. All that gold — and it's gonna be all ours!"

"So what're we waitin' for?" cackled Elmer.

"California, here we come!" Jed cried triumphantly.

In jubilation, he hurled the torn corset into the air. Upward it flew to lodge firmly in the V of a branch jutting from a tree-trunk. Jed re-wrapped the map in the oilskin, stowed it in his shirt and, in a matter of minutes, they were riding again, Elmer yelling a question.

"Whichaway is west?"

* * *

Four o'clock that afternoon, the ranch-hand known to folk in and around Masonville as Bobcat Jerry rode into town on his familiar appaloosa and made straight for the town jail fronted by the office of Marshal Ed Manders. Though a cattletown, there were few heavy duties here for pudgy Manders and his deputy. Local cowhands rarely indulged in payday hell-raising, unlike the bunkhouse gangs of spreads in the vicinity of Arnold City, the county seat. Underworked Deputy Town Marshal Marty Link was, therefore, as flabby as his boss, as much in need of exercise.

When the half-breed trudged in, the lawmen greeted him casually. Manders was slumped in his desk chair, Link seated at a table, absorbed in a week-old newspaper. Bobcat Jerry, though on the payroll of the Bracket 7 spread, was a known wanderer, having inherited the nomadic instincts of his redskin mother. He hunted, when not involved in chores around the ranch.

Grunting to himself, he moved

silently on moccasined feet to the rear wall on which were thumbtacked handbills adorned by pictures of lawbreakers under the bold type that read 'Wanted.'

"Seen 'em," he announced. "It was two and a half hours back and I seen 'em clear and, if I wasn't hid so good, they'd of spotted me and I'd be a dead'un now."

"Who'd you see, Jerry?" asked Manders, deciding he should show some interest.

"This'un for sure." A brown finger stabbed at a poster, then another. "And this'un. Ain't sure'bout all six of 'em, but three I seen clear, and this is two of 'em."

"Aw, hell, Marty," winced Manders. "He's pointin' at Reno Hamill and Johnny Deuce, a couple real mean ones. Six you say, Jerry?" The half-breed nodded vehemently. "Damn. The whole Hamill gang. Where'd you see 'em?"

Bobcat Jerry, the lawmen were told,

was some distance east of the settlement, he and his horse well concealed in a brush clump. His Sharps was lined on a plump jackrabbit and, lucky for him, he heard riders just as he was about to squeeze trigger. Being cautious by nature, he stayed put to watch a half-dozen horsemen move past, three of whom he had seen before.

"Not personal, huh Jerry?" prodded Link. "Just pictures of 'em?"

"Pictures," said the half-breed.

"You stay hid till they were out of sight?" demanded Manders. "Why am I askin' that? What else would you do? Well, whichaway were they headed?"

Bobcat Jerry gestured and the deputy was moved to curse bitterly.

"The Wells Fargo trail, Ed. Plain enough Hamill's fixin' to hit another stage."

"When's Western Union gonna string wire from here to the county seat?" grouched Manders. "We're town officers, got no authority beyond Masonville . . ."

"And we got no telegraph," scowled

Link, "else we could wire Sheriff McWade."

"Leo McWade could depute a posse strong enough to hunt Hamill and trap the whole gang, but we can't budge," complained Manders. The half-breed had turned from the wall and was moving restlessly about the office. "Jerry, you recognized three of 'em, but we got no bulletin on the third feller."

"Seen him," insisted Bobcat Jerry. "Seen his picture, but don't recall where," Then he paused by the table, bent to stare and startled the deputy by whisking the newspaper from his hands. "This'un! Damn right. This him."

"Lemme see," urged Manders. The newspaper was placed on his desk for his appraisal of the photographs under the banner headline: 'The Marchmount Heirs.' The brown finger jabbed at an inscrutable face and the marshal announced the name printed beneath it. "Clive M. Renfield. I don't believe this. He's kin to the late

Ellie Marchmount, widow of the most important Marchmount of 'em all, old Clute himself."

"Me sure," growled Bobcat Jerry.

About to support his boss's protest, Marty Link held his tongue and squinted perplexedly. On the one hand, he asked himself, why would a relative of the Marchmounts be riding with an outlaw as notorious, as elusive as Reno Hamill? On the other hand, Bobcat Jerry had eyes like an eagle's and a memory like an elephant's. When he made an identification, you could bet a month's pay on its accuracy.

"Mighty strange," sighed Manders. "One thing about you, Jerry. Nobody ever called you a liar . . ."

"Talk *straight*," the half-breed assured him.

" . . . and I ain't about to doubt your word," nodded Manders. "But it sure is the strangest thing I ever heard."

"Only thing we can do — and it don't seem much — is warn the crew

of the next coach passin' through,"
said Link.

"Next coach is the northeaster,"
frowned Manders. "They overnight
here." He grimaced and pointed out,
"After they leave tomorrow mornin',
their noon stop'll be Arnold City,
and chances are the Hamill bunch'll
be layin' for 'em somewheres between
here and the county seat." He grimaced
again as he got to his feet and donned
his hat. "I'm goin' along to the depot
and ask Abe if this rig's carryin'
cash, and who's gonna be on the
box this run."

At the Wells Fargo depot, the
balding, bewhiskered Abe Dolman,
manager here for five years or more,
listened to the marshal's repetition of
the half-breed's report. Then it was
his turn to bemoan the lack of
communication with the county seat.

"Every other time was different," he
said grimly. "We didn't know Hamill
was anywhere in this territory. This
time we know — and what the hell

can we do about it?"

"Any idea what Hamill's after, Abe?" asked Manders. "This northeaster carryin' valuables, a cash shipment, gold . . . ?"

"Passengers and mail and that's all," said Dolman. "And wait till I tell you who's drivin' and who's ridin' shotgun this run — Malone and Britt."

"Couple real hardnoses, them two," remarked Manders.

"Hamill's been getting away with murder and Harp and Joe hates his guts for it," fretted Dolman. "There was a guard name of Prendergast got gunned right off his seat by the Hamill gang about eight months ago, up along the north route to Lanesburg. And Prendergast, poor sonofagun, was a close buddy of Harp and Joe."

"I guess it's your duty to warn the passengers," said Manders.

"The crew has to be warned first," said Dolman. He checked his watch. "Stage'll arrive in about twenty-five minutes."

They moved out to the sidewalk. Manders lit a cigar and the depot-boss filled and lit his pipe. Almost twenty minutes later, while they were staring to the southwest, two horsemen materialized out of the heat haze. Soon, they were entering Masonville and idling their mounts along the street toward the Wells Fargo depot.

Manders and Dolman studied them curiously as they reined up in front of the depot. Larry jerked a thumb to indicate the hotel across the street.

"That where stage passengers stay tonight?" he asked.

"That's where," nodded Dolman. "Willet Hotel, best in town."

"Nearest livery stable?" drawled Stretch.

"You can see it from here," offered Manders, pointing. "Crockett's."

"Muchas gracias," said Larry.

"Coming in from the southwest, did you sight a stagecoach headed this way?" asked Dolman.

"Right behind us," Larry assured

him. "Ought to roll in any minute."

The Texans made for the livery stable and, soon afterward, the stage arrived. Manders stood by, watching depot hands unload baggage for transfer to the hotel and the passengers descending, stretching cramped limbs. When the last bag had been handed down, the crew dropped to the sidewalk to trade greetings with Dolman. Being allergic to lazy lawmen, they pointedly ignored Manders.

"Harp, Joe, bad news," Dolman said quietly.

"This information's mighty reliable," declared Manders.

"What information?" demanded Malone. "What's this all about?"

"We know for a fact the Hamill gang's in the area," muttered Dolman. "They were seen and three of them identified. Six in all, Harp, and headed northeast — and you know what *that* means."

"I want to hear more," decided Malone. Then he glanced over his shoulder. The tall men were half-way to the hotel from Crockett's barn, hefting their gear. "And we got a couple friends ought to hear it too."

"Those strangers?" frowned Dolman.

"To me and Harp, they ain't strangers," retorted Britt.

He whistled and beckoned and the Texans changed course, stepping off the opposite side-walk to cross the street diagonally. At Malone's urging, they followed the crew and the marshal into the depot office.

Manders again repeated everything told him by sharp-eyed Bobcat Jerry. Malone swore fluently; he was still swearing when his partner thought to name the tall men, and it pleased the trouble-shooters that, though Dolman knew them by reputation, the marshal did not.

Having exhausted his repertoire of profanity, Malone stared hard at Larry and asked,

"How d'you like this?"

"About as much as you, Harp,"

frowned Larry. He tugged at an ear and eyed Manders pensively. "This Renfield hombre, the 'breed's sure, huh?"

"One of the Marchmount heirs," said Manders. "Picture in a newspaper. Renfield, the Marchmount brothers and a lady name of Dobson."

"Glad you said 'lady'," muttered Larry. "That's just what she is."

"They got to be friends of ours, her and her man." said Stretch. "Runt, this don't set right with me."

"Makes four of us don't like the smell of it," said Larry. "Harp and Joe and us."

"Since there's a strong chance Hamill's planning another hold-up, Wells Fargo has a responsibility to the passengers," fretted Dolman.

"What're you supposed to do?" asked Larry.

"My duty to warn 'em and give 'em the option," said Dolman. "The stage rolls anyway eight-fifteen tomorrow morning. Any of them want to risk it, we can't stop them, but I'm hoping they'll listen to reason, take their own safety into account."

"Oughtn't be any of them travellers aboard," said Larry. "Specially the women. We might get an argument from Pete, but I figure I can talk him into stayin' behind with Kitty. Old man Dawson, he's kind of proddy . . . "

"But his wife, the big'un, wears the — you know what I mean," winced Stretch.

"We owe Hamill and his gunhawks, Joe and me," scowled Harp.

"I know how you feel, Harp, but it's plain the schedule has to be altered," frowned the depot-boss. "I mean, now that we have this information."

"We ought to use what we've found out, turn it against them bandidos," declared Larry. "Bad bunch, huh? Hit a lot of stagecoaches?"

"And banks," said Manders. "Been at it a long time. They're only seen when they go a'raidin'. Posses've tried trailin' 'em, but lose 'em everytime.

They cover their backtrail good and they got a hideout that's never been found."

"So the hell with it," growled Larry, staring hard at Malone and the guard. "We play this smart, we could nail 'em."

Britt grinned in grim relish.

"Trouble-shooter, Harp and me ain't fixin' to haul five passengers into an ambush," he muttered. "Two of 'em female means bad luck. But, if you got any ideas . . ."

Larry had an idea. Stretch would have been surprised if he hadn't. The idea was offered slowly and calmly, Larry making it sound simple, the marshal and the Wells Fargo men listening, sometimes trading glances. When he had said it all, Malone assured him,

"I know every mile of the trail from here to the county seat like I know my own face, includin' every rock, every patch of brush six bandidos could be hidin' in. It's a helluva plan you've handed us — and it could work."

"When me and Harp're expectin' trouble," declared Britt, "that's what makes the difference."

"We'll have an edge," enthused Malone.

"Bueno," grunted Larry. "We're the only ones know, okay?" He fixed an eye on Manders. "Don't even tell your deputy."

"Marty's reliable," protested Manders.

"We're playin' for high stakes," Larry retorted. "The 'breed saw six of 'em. How do we know there ain't a seventh — right here in Masonville?"

"A spy?" blinked Manders.

"Why take dumb risks?" challenged Larry. "A word in the wrong place could tip our hand."

"All right, so only us six're in on the plan," agreed Manders. "But Marty and me got no authority anywhere but right here in town. We'd both come along with you if we could. Policin' the county is Leo McWade's responsibility, him bein' county sheriff."

"Don't you fret none," leered Britt.

"Four of us can get the job done," opined Malone. "Road agents don't like surprises — and we're gonna spring a doozy on 'em."

"You talk to the Dawsons and the drummer", Larry told the depot-boss. "It better be my partner and me parleys with Kitty and her man."

"You're thinking she'll take it bad," guessed Dolman. "A Marchmount riding with the Hamill gang."

"I don't know how she'll take it," shrugged Larry. "Depends how she feels about cousin Clive."

"Better not tell her over supper," Stretch suggested as they picked up their gear. "Later?"

"Later," nodded Larry.

"Guess I'll follow your example," decided Dolman, "give the other three time to eat and settle down before I explain things."

The tall men checked into a ground-floor double at the Willet Hotel in time to join the Dobson's for supper.

Kitty and her husband aimed friendly smiles as they joined them and, over that meal, Larry kept them talking about P-Bar-D and their plans for its development. If he and his partner were preoccupied, the young couple didn't notice. The ruse by which they had rid themselves of two clumsy miscreants bent on purloining Kitty's corset was discussed to the accompaniment of subdued laughter; both Dobsons were still enjoying the joke.

When they were lingering over their coffee, Pete dropped his voice to assure the Texans,

"We aren't foolish enough to brag of Kitty's inheritance, the real inheritance I mean. I wouldn't insult you good friends by . . . "

"You don't have to say it, Pete," Larry assured him. "A map to a fortune's like a short fuse on a can of gunpowder. You keep it a secret as careful as you keep that can far clear of a campfire."

"And so much has to be arranged,"

murmured Kitty. "An expedition into the Sierra Nevada, equipment, pack-animals and things we'd need to know — the location of the nearest bank for instance."

"Three men, meanin' Pete and us," Stretch said flatly. "I'd figure four pack-critters maybe, and we'd need provisions, tools and such."

"You're already offering . . . ?" began Pete.

"Hey," Larry said with a wry grin. "You'll need protection and the right kind of company, a couple hombres you can trust. How else could it work?"

"You'd do all that for us?" frowned Kitty.

"Any reason we oughtn't?" shrugged Stretch. "We got nothin' better to do."

"But, speakin' of insults, just don't offer us a percentage of the stash," warned Larry. "You already know we got no use for mucho dinero and, besides, it's Kitty's inheritance we're talkin' about. The way we see it, it's

225

long past time you young folks got prosperous."

"It seems we're to be grateful to you the rest of our lives," Kitty said wistfully.

"I don't reckon you'll be grateful for what we got to tell you after supper," muttered Larry.

"Meaning?" prodded Pete.

"Time for another parley, just you and us," said Larry. "Somethin' we've found out, somethin' Kitty has to know. But this ain't the time nor place. Your room, when we're through here."

In their room a little while later, the young couple sat side by side on the bed, holding hands and watching the tall men straddling chairs and building smokes, Pete curious, his wife disquieted by Larry's expression.

He led off by asking her a question, at once regretting it had to be put so bluntly.

# 8

## Attack And Counter-Attack

KITTY'S eyebrows shot up. The question surprised her, but she rallied quickly.

"How well do I know Clive Renfield? Not closely, I'm glad to say. Relatives should get along . . . "

"If they can," Pete interjected.

" . . . but I've nothing in common with him and I can't be a hyprocrite," she went on. "I don't like his style and — and I can't imagine my uncle and aunt were ever fond of him."

"Black sheep of the family?" asked Larry.

"A wastrel," she said bitterly. "He spends all his time in low class districts of Sacramento, haunting the gambling dens. He's a show-off and no gentleman."

"Tinhorn," growled Pete.

"Makes it a mite easier, huh runt?" Stretch said in relief.

"Makes it a whole lot easier," remarked Larry. "Kitty, you said there was talk of the Sierra Stash when the will was read?"

"Brad and Sam were surprised it wasn't mentioned," she nodded. "But they're already so wealthy it was no big disappointment to them. Cousin Clive? I declare he was downright feverish. All he inherited was Uncle Clute's clothes, and he tore every garment.

"Hoping to find the map in the lining of a coat, a pocket maybe, or stuck in a boot," recalled Pete. "What about Renfield, Larry?"

"He ain't in Sacramento," said Larry. Then he repeated all he and Stretch and the stage crew had been told in the Wells Fargo office, emphasizing that the Hamill gang was notorious in this general region and, in conclusion, warning, "It don't take much brainwork to figure what's gonna happen manana

228

somewheres 'tween Masonville and Arnold City. Why else would Renfield throw in with an owlhoot bunch? So, when the stage rolls, you won't be aboard. There'll be no passengers aboard."

"Just us," Stretch said casually. "And the crew'll carry us for free. We don't need to buy passage."

"Depot-boss'll be talkin' to the other passengers," offered Larry.

"Why does it have to be just you and the crew?" demanded Pete. "How about volunteers — an escort party?"

"Pete, it's a chance to stop a real mean bandido," countered Larry.

"Cunning jasper," Stretch pointed out. "Him and his buddies spot an escort party, they'll back off."

"We don't want 'em to back off," declared Larry. "When they make their play, we'll be ready for 'em. Four against six ain't rough odds for us, and we'll have the edge on 'em. Surprise tactics win the game every time. We know. We've worked this trick before."

"A time or two," Stretch said modestly.

"I'm a fair hand with my Colt," muttered Pete. "I should be with you."

"Pete . . . !" began Kitty.

"It's for us they're gonna risk their lives, honey," he protested. "It just doesn't seem fair."

"Amigo, I can tell you two good reasons you'll stay here with your wife," said Larry. "First reason, she'd fret herself sick about you every minute you were gone. Second reason, we'd be sidetracked havin' you along, worryin' about coverin' you, keepin' you alive. In a shootin' fight, that's somethin' we *don't* need."

"Need to keep our minds on business," shrugged Stretch. "In any kind of showdown, a man has to — you know — concentrate?"

"Pete, they're right," Kitty said urgently. "They have to do it their way."

Pete had to agree, albeit reluctantly.

"Decoys you'll be," he frowned.

"Not for the first time," said Larry. "And don't fret on our account. The driver and guard're rarin' to go and this is our kind of action. We know what to do and how to do it."

"What if they notice the coach is empty?" asked Pete.

"Malone says we'll be raisin' a lot of dust this time of year," said Larry. "If the dust shades on the windows're down, it'll seem natural, no way they'll guess there's only one of us inside." He nodded to his partner. They got to their feet. "Might's well turn in early. Longer we sleep, the sharper we'll be manana."

"You'll have breakfast with us — please?" begged Kitty. "And I'll pray — it won't be for the last time."

"Hey, you ain't seen the last of us," grinned Larry. "We aim to stay alive and healthy. Don't forget we promised to side Pete all the way to your Uncle Clute's cache."

By the time the Texans were calling it a day, the Dawsons and Noah Beasley had been advised they would be staying longer than expected in Masonville. Wells Fargo's apologies for the delay, but normal service would be resumed within twenty-four hours; Abe Dolman fervently hoped this estimate would prove correct.

★ ★ ★

8.10 of the following morning, after breakfasting with the Dobsons, the Texans quit the hotel toting only their Winchesters; upon waking, they had cleaned, oiled and loaded those weapons, their sidearms also.

The coach was in readiness in front of the depot, team in harness, Malone and Britt in position and wearing expressions best described as hopeful; it was clear that, if they failed to encounter road agents this morning, they would be bitterly disappointed. As they approached, Larry flicked a glance to the vehicle's roof to assure himself a certain item had not been forgotten.

"Whose baggage?" he asked Dolman. "Looks a mite toilworn."

"Just cover for you," muttered the depot-boss. "I picked 'em up last night, second-hand, packed some hard stuff in them, rocks and such. Might shield you from a bullet with your name on it. But not heavy enough to bother the team if Harp has to make speed."

"What d'you mean — if?" grinned Stretch, raising his rifle stock-first. "Like to borrow this, Joe? From inside, I'll do good enough with my hoglegs."

"Winchester," the guard noted as he accepted it. "Loaded for bear?"

"For buzzards," said Stretch.

Britt chuckled grimly and said,

"That's the right word for what I hope to be shootin'."

"Get aboard, boys," urged Malone. "I'll stop a little way out of town for you, Larry."

The Texans climbed in. Malone kicked off the brake and cussed the team and the rig rolled out of

Masonville and onto the regular trail. After a quarter-mile, the vehicle was stalled where the route cut through tall timber. Larry dropped from it, tossed his rifle to the roof, then clambered up there. The baggage had been lashed either side, permitting him to lie prone with the tarp concealing him. He readied his rifle and coolly announced,

"Okay, I'm set. Let's go."

As the stage rolled on, Stretch made himself comfortable, resting his bootheels on the opposite seat. Up top, Britt nursed his shotgun and kept the taller Texans's rifle at his feet. Malone, driving with the expertise born of long practice, kept his gaze on the territory ahead and assured the decoys,

"I'll give you plenty warnin' when we're nearin' likely stakeouts."

The ambush site nominated by Reno Hamill was seventeen miles southwest of Arnold City, the noon stop. The bend was sharp, almost right-angular, demanding that drivers approaching from either direction should reduce speed for the turn. High rocks provided ample cover for six mounted men with, a little way east of the stakeout, a stretch of brush.

"They slow down less'n forty-five yards from here," the boss-bandit calmly informed Renfield.

"Sure," nodded Berman. "No driver ever took this bend at speed."

"Johnny, Slim, get a clear bead on the shotgun," drawled Hamill. "He gets his before we break cover."

"Just like that, huh?" challenged Renfield.

"Reno's first rule," Berman remarked with a callous grin. "Never give a shotgun guard any kind of chance."

"The driver'll stop," Hamill predicted. "Then we invite Renfield's cousin to climb out and, if her lovin' husband tries anything, he'll be next to go."

"Him and any passenger shows a gun," growled Williams.

"Hell, what've we got to lose?" muttered Johnny Deuce. "The Sierra

Stash is what, and I crave my cut of it."

"Last time out for us, Reno," mused Slim Raitt.

"The big one," grinned Hamill.

"Damn right," nodded Raitt. "Rich men don't need to pull no more hold-ups."

"Feelin' a chill in your gut?" Hamill asked Renfield. "Gettin' edgy about what we're gonna do to your cousin?"

"All I care about is *my* share of the old man's gold," Renfield assured him.

"We gonna draw straws to decide who's gonna tear her duds off and separate her from that corset-thing?" leered Williams.

"When the time comes, don't fight about it, boys," chuckled Hamill. "Just get it done fast."

At 9.45 Malone warned his partner, "Timber comin' up on your side."

"I'm watchin' it," said Britt.

They passed the timber without challenge. Ten minutes later, approaching a curve of the trail, Malone eased back on his reins, but just enough for a slight slowdown. No danger of an ambush here, no cover either side. Caution was observed a quarter-hour later when the trail wound round the base of a butte but, again, the crew saw no cause to alert the Texans.

Another twenty minutes and the sharp bend became visible and, to eagle-eyed Britt, something else.

"He ducked," he called loud enough for the decoys to hear. "But not fast enough. Only caught a glimpse . . . "

"But you're certain-sure?" demanded Malone.

"Certain-sure," insisted Britt. "The rocks is where they're waitin' for us."

"Few more minutes and they'll look for me to slow down," Malone called to their passengers. "But there'll be no slow down, not this time. Ain't much of that brush right of the rocks. I'm swingin' these critters right off the trail and straight through the brush — which is just what they ain't expectin'. That'll put us on the trail again other side of the bend."

"They'll chase us for sure," grinned Britt.

"And what's yonder of the bend?" Larry demanded.

"Five miles of straight trail across flat ground — flat and wide open!" announced Malone.

"No cover for 'em if they try to catch up with us," declared Britt.

"Sounds good to me," yelled Larry. "How about you, beanpole?"

From within the vehicle, Stretch replied,

"I ain't complainin'."

"Hang on," growled Malone. Couple more minutes and we cut for the brush."

Edging half of his face around a rock, Hamill followed the approach of the speeding vehicle.

"Right on time," he commented.

"You can always rely on Wells Fargo," drawled Berman. "Always. punctual."

"Johnny — Slim . . . " said Hamill. Deuce and Raitt readied their rifles.

"Aim good," urged Williams. "One of you misses, the other won't."

"Driver'll slow the team right about — now," announced Hamill. Then he loosed an oath. "Is he loco?"

"What's happening?" demanded Renfield.

"Sonofabitch!" gasped Raitt. "He's swinging off the trail to drive clear through the brush!"

"And he ain't slowin' down!" raged Williams.

"Smart-ass," scowled Hamill. "He could make it to the trail again, but that won't help him any."

At his command, the ambushers wheeled their mounts to descend from their vantage-point while, at full speed, Malone drove through brush too fragile to impede his hard-running team. Out of the brush and nearing the trail again, driver and guard darted glances to their left, spotting the six bandana-masked horsemen breaking from the rocks. Britt

239

did exactly as the outlaws expected, discharging one barrel of his shotgun as a deterrent bound to be ignored.

When the coach was on the trail and speeding across the flats, Stretch rolled up the flaps, emptied his holsters and removed his Stetson. He glanced out and backward while, on the roof, Larry began thrusting his canvas covering aside. The outlaws were in hot pursuit now. Rifles and six-guns barked, the reports echoing across the flats. Bullets sped past Malone, hunched on his seat now, urging his three spans to greater speed.

Larry chose a target and triggered his first shot. The rider veered slightly. First shot from the defenders, first miss; the move saved that raider's life — temporarily. Now Britt turned on his seat armed not with his shotgun but with Stretch's Winchester, loosed a yell of defiance and got off two fast ones and, leaning out a rightside window, Stretch drew a bead on a rider with his lefthand Colt. His weapon boomed in unison with the bark of his partner's rifle and the pursuers were suddenly reduced by two. Stretch's target was driven from his saddle by the impact of a .45 slug hitting him dead centre. The rider winged by Larry cried out in shock and anguish, dropped his pistol and, with his right shoulder bloody, toppled, fell and rolled.

"Keep it up!" bellowed Malone. "They're still comin'!"

A rider came up at a hard gallop, making for the left side of the speeding coach, rising in his stirrups to aim his rifle at the driver. Larry made sure of that one. His Winchester barked and another saddle emptied.

His force halved, Hamill cursed obscenely and yelled to the two still mounted.

"Flank the coach! Aim for the horses!"

The command came loud enough for the Texans to hear over the clamor of pounding hooves. As the other two began closing the gap, spurring their animals mercilessly, Larry took sight on Hamill, who was in handgun range now, his Colt levelled. The six-gun boomed and the slug plowed into woodwork inches under Larry's propped elbow, but did not deflect his arm. He triggered and put Hamill out of the fight. The boss-bandit back-somersaulted over his horse's rump to hit ground in an ugly heap.

Simultaneously, Stretch and Britt fired at the rider coming up right of them, his weapon aimed at the front right team-horse. They both scored and the man's gun discharged, but skyward, as he keeled from his mount.

Responding to a warning yell from his partner, Stretch threw himself to a leftside window with both hands gunfilled. The last of the greed-crazed six was about to level his rifle at the team when Stretch roared a challenge. As the rifle swung toward him, he discharged his matched .45s and, at that short range, the force of two bullets slamming into him was more than enough to knock the man off his horse.

"Slow down some, Harp!" called Larry. "Turn back and we'll check for survivors! Stretch, when the rig's close enough, jump out and head off a horse!"

"You read my mind," Stretch replied. "I don't aim to round up them critters afoot." He thrust his head out again. "Harp? Joe?"

"We're fine," the driver growled as he wheeled the team. "Couple times there, we near got our heads blowed off, but . . ."

"Too close for comfort," said Britt. "Not close enough to score on us. We won, by damn!"

Malone drove back slowly and, when the rig was level with the last raider to fall, the taller Texan jumped out and approached the riderless animal, calling to it cajolingly. He was mounted by the time the coach came to a halt and Larry climbed down from the roof.

Drawing and cocking his Colt, Larry

moved warily to the well-separated figures of the fallen. He checked on a dead man and, as he moved on to the next, heard a voice raised in fear and agony.

"Help me, Herb! Where the hell are you? I'm wounded — in pain . . . !"

"That's Renfield wailin'," the dying Slim Raitt mumbled as Larry hunkered beside him. "I — had a hunch — if it come to a fight — he'd show yellow . . . "

He breathed his last after that contemptuous utterance. Grim-faced, Larry trudged on to the other prone figures, while his partner did an expert job of mustering the riderless animals. Soon, he was dropping to one knee by the only survivor, who clasped at his bloody right shoulder and pleaded frantically.

"A doctor! Don't let me — bleed to death — damn it! Get me to a doctor!"

"I won't let you die, Renfield," Larry sourly promised. "I plan on diggin' that slug out and patchin' you the best way

I know how, because I hanker for you to stand trial — you no-good sonofabitch."

"My name — isn't Renfield!" gasped the wounded man.

"Tinhorn, if you want to keep your name a secret," jibed Larry, "never get your picture in a newspaper."

The stage crew descended to help Stretch lash dead men onto horses. Watched by Malone, Larry sterilized the blade of his jack-knife with whiskey found in a saddlebag and began probing for the bullet in the fleshy part of Renfield's shoulder. Renfield loosed one howl and fainted and, a few moments later, the slug had been removed and Larry was saturating the wound with whiskey and calling for bandanas, shirttails, any material be could use to improvise a dressing and bandage.

"We're closer to the county seat than anywhere else?" he asked.

Malone consulted his watch and calculated,

"We could make Arnold City by one o'clock." He nodded brusquely to the still-unconscious survivor. "If he ain't leakin' blood no more, he can travel in the rig."

"Yeah, okay," nodded Larry. "With one of them saddle-animals totin' two stiffs, Stretch and me'll have mounts. You lead. We'll follow you in."

Arnold City was bigger than Tealsburg and three times the size of Masonville. With the northeastbound stage a full forty-five minutes late, the local Wells Fargo representative was sharing the porch of the county law office with the lean and austere Sheriff Leo McWade and his senior deputy, squatly-built and swarthy, Elmann by name. The lawmen and the depot-manager, Jesse Hill, were reacting predictably, swapping theories as to why the noon coach was behind schedule.

"Let's not fear the worst," muttered Hill. "Harness is checked regularly, wheels and axles too, but there's always the chance of a breakdown. For all we know, it could've happened before this rig made Masonville."

"By the end of the year," offered the deputy.

"What?" frowned Hill.

"By the end of the year," Elmann repeated. "That's what Colborn told me at the Western Union office. They'll have wire strung to Masonville so, in time of trouble, Manders can telegraph us."

"Any chance one of the crew took sick?" asked McWade.

"It'll be Malone and Britt this run," said Hill. "I don't say they're youngters, both of them getting on, truth to tell. But sick? No." Despite his apprehension, he grinned. "Those two are too ornery to get sick. It'd take pneumonia or a bullet to stop them getting through."

"Speakin' of bullets," drawled Elmann. "If nobody else is gonna say it, I'll say it. Hamill gang's still on the loose. My money says this coach got ambushed. Any takers?"

"Damn Hamill," scowled McWade. "I got just one ambition, something I crave to settle before I retire. We find clear tracks to Hamill's hideaway hole — and take the bastard."

Hill heaved a sigh of relief and pointed.

"Dust," he said.

He and the lawmen stared southwest beyond the big town's outskirts where some two hundred yards of the stage trail was visible from their vantage-point. Two minutes passed before the familiar vehicle and its six-horse team materialized, and then McWade was observing,

"Riders tagging."

"What can that mean?" wondered Hill.

"We'd best wait at the depot," said McWade, leading them to the porch steps.

Other locals, among them the daughter and the two sons of the Dawsons, waited with Hill and the lawmen out front of the stage depot. The daughter remarked to McWade,

"If the Hamill gang held up this stage, their ears'll still be burning. Ma would've bawled them out for sure."

"All I hope is Pa didn't try for a shot at them," fretted her elder brother. "He's too ready to pull that old pistol of his — and can't hit any target because he always forgets to put his spectacles on."

From the end of Main Street, the coach steadily approached the depot with two riders following, leading laden horses. Then Harp Malone was hauling back on his reins and loudly announcing,

"The Hamill gang's wiped out — all but one! We decoyed 'em, by golly!"

"Hell's bells!" breathed the depot-manager.

"Recognize them two?" Elmann asked his boss, as the Texans reined up.

"Damn right," nodded McWade. "And, if Hamill was lured into some kind of trap, you can bet your badge it wasn't Malone's idea."

"Only one party inside," called Britt, as he climbed down. "Only one of 'em still livin'. Larry got his name."

The Dawsons raised their voices, anxiously questioning Malone. Larry reassured them.

"Safe back in Masonville with the other passengers. We couldn't risk havin' 'em aboard on account of we were ninety percent sure we'd have a run-in with Hamill." He eyed the lawmen. "Which of you's sheriff here?"

"I am, Valentine," said McWade.

"Bueno," grunted Larry. "You're gonna need a doc and a JP at the county jail and an undertaker to tend Hamill and the other stiffs. My partner and me'll fetch the prisoner."

"Plain enough you savvy the procedure," grinned Elmann.

"Oh, sure," sighed Stretch. "We've done it all before, answered all the questions, put our names to affidavits. It's kind of teejus, but we know it's got to be done."

"Jesse, soon as we eat, soon as you have the boys hitch a fresh team, I'm takin' this rig back to Masonville," said Malone. "We'll overnight there and that'll foul up the schedule, but . . ."

"Don't worry, I'll wire all stops northeast," said Hill.

"It'll save time if you eat at my office," decided McWade. "I'll need statements from you and Britt too. Deputy Yates'll have a cafe deliver the food. Let's go, boys."

In the sheriff's office, the Texans and the stage crew talked and satisfied their appetites, a JP scribbling urgently, an Arnold City medico attending Renfield in a cell. Making his statement, explaining all the salient points, Larry discreetly refrained from mention of the map to the Sierra Stash and its unusual hiding place out of respect for Kitty Dobson's right to privacy. The way he told it, Renfield must have had his own reasons for throwing in with the Hamill gang and becoming an accomplice in an armed robbery attempt.

How much would Renfield say when questioned? The trouble-shooters figured that was pretty much up to him. And they weren't concerned. With Malone and Britt backing their account of the running fight, Renfield was undoubtedly an accessory. The crime having been attempted inside Arnold County, he would stand trial here and odds against a not guilty verdict were insurmountable. As sure as there were cattle in Texas, the black sheep of the Marchmount clan would spend a big part of the rest of his life in a state penitentiary.

When the heroes were through eating and all statements signed and witnessed, the sheriff presented them with Havana cigars and made a brief speech.

"Some law officers would resent what you tumblewoods have achieved this day. County and Federal lawmen all over the state were after the Hamill gang, hungering to locate his hideout."

"Don't feel bad about it," drawled

Stretch, after burping contentedly. "If no posse ever found the hideout, I don't reckon me and my partner could've. Hell, we ain't special and it's for sure we can't work miracles. We're human like every other son."

"Somehow, Hamill was lured from his hideout to hold up another stage," frowned McWade.

"One time too many," grinned Britt. "Six of the sonsabitches. But, with Larry on the roof with his rifle, Stretch inside with his Colts and me and Harp up top — we had 'em outnumbered."

"And out-classed," Malone said with relish. "But that's enough gab. Anything else you want from us, Sheriff?"

"I'd like to finish my little speech to these fiddlefoots — you mind?" challenged McWade.

"Make it quick," urged Malone. "Them and us hanker to get back to Masonville before dark."

"I'm not a jealous man," McWade told the Texans. "I don't resent your latest victory. On behalf of the

253

lawmen and citizens of every town on the northeast route, I'm thanking you — and congratulating you."

"Forget it," shrugged Larry.

"It was no trouble at all," said Stretch.

At this point, the editor of the Arnold County *Clarion* came bustling in to seek an interview with the notorious trouble-shooters, who responded by inviting him to go leap off a high roof.

Obviously, this was the right time for the Texans to return to the depot, board the coach and be transported back to Masonville by the jubilant Malone and Britt.

★ ★ ★

Around 8.30 that night, another get-together in the Dobson room at the Willet Hotel, Masonville. Kitty and her husband listened to the trouble-shooters' account of the running fight and the defeat of the outlaw gang without interrupting and, to Larry's relief, reacted fatalistically to the full significance of Clive Renfield's treachery.

"I hoped for just enough for our needs," she said softly. "Not a fortune, not Uncle Clute's cache of gold."

"Renfield wanted it so bad . . . " Pete winced in disgust, "he turned for help to the most lowdown outlaw in all Nevada. Nothing he wouldn't have done to get his paws on Kitty's map."

"How could I feel sorry for him?" she murmured. "If we'd been killed, he couldn't have cared." She eyed Larry thoughtfully. "He must've guessed the map was hidden in . . . ?"

"That's how it seems to me," nodded Larry. "And, when he made that guess — like Pete said — there's nothin' he wouldn't have done."

"He sure proved *that*," muttered Stretch.

"We owe you so much," sighed Kitty.

"Don't start thankin' us," shrugged

Stretch. "Larry and me, we say the job ain't finished yet."

"You mean to go all the way with me?" prodded Pete.

"All the way," Larry assured him. "When Kitty's safe back at P-Bar-D, you and us're headed straight west to California again, the high country. The map'll lead us to the cache and, by then we'll have pack-critters. Whole thing has to be handled quiet. We just load the gold and make for the nearest bank."

"Scudder Creek's only a small place, but we do have a lawyer there and a bank too," offered Kitty. "I could arrange for Pete to have a document giving him the right to act for me. It's called a power of attorney."

"Sure," nodded Pete. "That's all I'll need for trading the gold for cash. And I won't have to carry all that money home. A California bank can fix up a draft on our bank at Scudder Creek."

"Sounds okay," approved Larry. "Meantime, it stays a secret, savvy?

We say nothin' to nobody in case some scribbler gets wise."

"Scribbler?" frowned Pete.

"Newspaper scribblers," growled Stretch. "A secret ain't a secret after *they* get to hear of it."

"Time enough for the news to spread all over the doggone country," Larry pointed out, "after your fortune's safe in the bank back home."

"I got just one thing to say," mumbled Stretch. "'Scuse me." He apologized to Kitty. "Your Aunt Ellie picked the strangest place to hide that map."

Two months later, the search of the three men investigating a remote area of the Sierra Nevada came to an end. The indications on the map drawn better than two decades before by Cluther Marchmount were clear enough. In a grove they found the flat rock, the right grove, the rock so accurately drawn by Kitty's kinsman. After securing their horses and the pack-animals, Pete Dobson and the

Texans improvised a crowbar of a stout limb cut from a pine, trimmed of foliage and with one end axed to a point.

Old Clute had stashed his nest-egg as a younger man and long ago; the rock had settled. The pointed end was rammed under the near side of the embedded slab. Then, with all three men bearing down on the limb, it budged and began rising. They forced downward till the rock rose and turned over, revealing the hole.

"Look at it," muttered Pete. "He stowed the stuff in leather sacks just big enough for one man to tote."

Larry lifted a sack out, unknotted the thongs at its neck and displayed the contents. He and his partner stayed cold calm, but the younger man's eyes popped.

"All right, that's it," said Larry. "Now we load it and take the down trail to Santa Rosa."

Within three days, a Santa Rosa assayer had finished testing and valuating the nuggets and the equivalent cash was deposited in the local branch of the Western & Pacific Bank for transfer by draft to the Dobsons' account at Scudder Creek. There in Santa Rosa, Pete warmly thanked the drifters and urged them travel home with him; if they would accept no financial remuneration for all their help, how about some P-Bar-D hospitality, a rest period, taking their ease at Scudder Creek for as long as they wished?

The trouble-shooters decided this was an offer too good to refuse.

A week later, a pig farmer whose homestead was located in high country some sixty miles from the site of the Sierra Stash travelled into the township of Purdy's Peak to buy supplies and a newspaper and lodge a complaint with the local law. A bemused Deputy Orin Coulter gave Alvin Brickett his full attention, after which he conceded,

"That's a damn peculiar thing, Alvin. I never heard the like."

"Worse'n peculiar," complained

Brickett. "They just keep diggin' that damn hole — on my land. Florrie and the kids're leery of 'em on accounta they pack six-guns and, come to that, the pigs don't like 'em neither. That hole, I swear it just gets bigger and wider and deeper and — consarn 'em — if it gets any *deeper* . . . !"

"Guess I better travel back with you," decided Coulter. It's your land, which makes 'em trespassers, so I can order 'em to leave."

Riding out of town, ambling his mount level with the seat of the pig farmer's wagon, the deputy asked if the intruders had addressed each other by name.

"Dunno their family monikers," grouched Brickett. "But one's called Jed and the other'un's called Elmer."

Being cautious by nature, Coulter eased his Colt in its holster when they reached the farm. Brickett climbed down with the newspaper tucked under an arm and called to his wife and

260

children watching from the farmhouse porch.

"Florrie, you and the young'uns stay inside. I brung the deputy like you can see. He'll roust 'em outa there."

"He better get 'em outa there fast," warned Florrie. "Them lunatics'll be buried alive if that dirt shifts." She pointed in agitation. "Look at it!"

Coulter needed no direction. The site of the excavation was all too obvious, marked by a high mound of earth fifteen feet south of a pen in which hogs grunted uneasily. Brickett followed him to the edge of the deep — the very deep — hole. He stared down at a couple of exhausted fanatics who hadn't shaved in weeks, whose clothes were tattered and dirt-smeared, one plying a pickaxe, the other a spade.

"Just what d'you two-legged gophers think you're doin'?" Coulter bellowed down to them.

"None of your dad-blamed business," came Jed's retort.

"Look up," ordered Coulter. "Look at my badge — then climb out of there in the name of the law."

As the scarecrows began struggling up the near side, the skinny one's companion gasped a challenge.

"How do we know that hunk o' tin's genuine? You could be a claim-jumper."

"You crazy or somethin'?" blinked Coulter. "Claim-jumper? No gold in this part of the mountains, no mines, no nothin'."

Crawling out of their hole, the scarecrows gawked at the newspapers's front page. Brickett, in the act of switching it to his other arm, had let it unfold. The headline taunted them mercilessly.

"Sonofabitch!" cried Jed. "It says . . . !"

"What — this?" Brickett studied the paper. "Oh, you mean the Marchmount gold, the Sierra Stash?"

"Old news," said the deputy. "Map to the cache was willed to a woman name of Dobson. Her husband and a couple drifters recovered it weeks ago. Those Dobsons're plenty rich now." He frowned perplexedly. "You *must* be crazy, if you've been diggin' for the cache so far from where it was found."

"What about this hole?" demanded Brickett.

"You two." Coulter gestured commandingly to the haggard duo. "Fill it in. Get to work with shovels and put all that earth back where you dug it from."

Jed's anguished exclamation and Elmer's shocked rejoinder were to mystify Coulter and the pig farmer for the rest of their lives.

"Aw, hell, Elmer! We got the wrong map!"

"And the wrong damn corset!"

# Epilogue

DURING 1932, the Depression period, two out of work saw-millers named Marsh and White, desperate for a dollar, were collaborating in the muscle-wearing chore of felling trees in the Southwest Nevada area and reducing them to firewood which they peddled to the citizenry of towns thereabouts.

On one such expedition, the younger of the two extricated something from a just-felled tree and exhibited it to his partner.

"Hey, Len. Hell's sakes — what d'you make of this?"

"Dave," frowned March. "What've you got there?"

"Listen, I could be wrong, but I'd swear . . . " began White.

"I'd swear too," said Marsh, making a close inspection. "And we'd both be right. That — or what's left of it — used to be a corset."

"That's what it looks like to me," chuckled White. "You realise how old it could be? Damn it, Len, it's the kind women used way back before the turn of the century."

"Uh huh." Marsh grunted in agreement. "Whalebone. But it ain't worth anything to us, friend, so toss it away and let's get to cuttin'."

White threw the tattered undergarment away and, before reaching for his axe, grinned and remarked.

"If that old corset could talk, I wonder what a story it could tell."

# THE DUDE MUST DIE
# WAIT FOR THE JUDGE
# HOLD 'EM BACK!

## FIGHTING RAMROD
### Charles N. Heckelmann

Most men would have cut their losses, but Frazer counted the bullets in his guns and said he'd soak the range in blood before he'd give up another inch of what was his.

## LONE GUN
### Eric Allen

Smoke Blackbird had been away too long. The Lequires had seized the Blackbird farm, forcing the Indians and settlers off, and no one seemed willing to fight! He had to fight alone.

## THE THIRD RIDER
### Barry Cord

Mel Rawlins wasn't going to let anything stand in his way. His father was murdered, his two brothers gone. Now Mel rode for vengeance.

## ARIZONA DRIFTERS
### W. C. Tuttle

When drifting Dutton and Lonnie Steelman decide to become partners they find that they have a common enemy in the formidable Thurston brothers.

## TOMBSTONE
### Matt Braun

Wells Fargo paid Luke Starbuck to outgun the silver-thieving stagecoach gang at Tombstone. Before long Luke can see the only thing bearing fruit in this eldorado will be the gallows tree.

## HIGH BORDER RIDERS
### Lee Floren

Buckshot McKee and Tortilla Joe cut the trail of a border tough who was running Mexican beef into Texas. They stopped the smuggler in his tracks.

## BRETT RANDALL, GAMBLER
### E. B. Mann

Larry Day had the choice of running away from the law or of assuming a dead man's place. No matter what he decided he was bound to end up dead.

## THE GUNSHARP
### William R. Cox

The Eggerleys weren't very smart. They trained their sights on Will Carney and Arizona's biggest blood bath began.

## THE DEPUTY OF SAN RIANO
### Lawrence A. Keating and
### Al. P. Nelson

When a man fell dead from his horse, Ed Grant was spotted riding away from the scene. The deputy sheriff rode out after him and came up against everything from gunfire to dynamite.

## FARGO: MASSACRE RIVER
### John Benteen

The ambushers up ahead had now blocked the road. Fargo's convoy was a jumble, a perfect target for the insurgents' weapons!

## SUNDANCE: DEATH IN THE LAVA
### John Benteen

The Modoc's captured the wagon train and its cargo of gold. But now the halfbreed they called Sundance was going after it . . .

## HARSH RECKONING
### Phil Ketchum

Five years of keeping himself alive in a brutal prison had made Brand tough and careless about who he gunned down . . .

## FARGO: PANAMA GOLD
### John Benteen

With foreign money behind him, Buckner was going to destroy the Panama Canal before it could be completed. Fargo's job was to stop Buckner.

## FARGO:
## THE SHARPSHOOTERS
### John Benteen

The Canfield clan, thirty strong were raising hell in Texas. Fargo was tough enough to hold his own against the whole clan.

## PISTOL LAW
### Paul Evan Lehman

Lance Jones came back to Mustang for just one thing — revenge! Revenge on the people who had him thrown in jail.

## HELL RIDERS
### Steve Mensing

Wade Walker's kid brother, Duane, was locked up in the Silver City jail facing a rope at dawn. Wade was a ruthless outlaw, but he was smart, and he had vowed to have his brother out of jail before morning!

## DESERT OF THE DAMNED
### Nelson Nye

The law was after him for the murder of a marshal — a murder he didn't commit. Breen was after him for revenge — and Breen wouldn't stop at anything . . . blackmail, a frameup . . . or murder.

## DAY OF THE COMANCHEROS
### Steven C. Lawrence

Their very name struck terror into men's hearts — the Comancheros, a savage army of cutthroats who swept across Texas, leaving behind a bloodstained trail of robbery and murder.

# SUNDANCE: SILENT ENEMY
## John Benteen

A lone crazed Cheyenne was on a personal war path. They needed to pit one man against one crazed Indian. That man was Sundance.

# LASSITER
## Jack Slade

Lassiter wasn't the kind of man to listen to reason. Cross him once and he'll hold a grudge for years to come — if he let you live that long.

# LAST STAGE TO GOMORRAH
## Barry Cord

Jeff Carter, tough ex-riverboat gambler, now had himself a horse ranch that kept him free from gunfights and card games. Until Sturvesant of Wells Fargo showed up.

## McALLISTER ON THE COMANCHE CROSSING
### Matt Chisholm

The Comanche, McAllister owes them a life — and the trail is soaked with the blood of the men who had tried to outrun them before.

## QUICK-TRIGGER COUNTRY
### Clem Colt

Turkey Red hooked up with Curly Bill Graham's outlaw crew. But wholesale murder was out of Turk's line, so when range war flared he bucked the whole border gang alone . . .

## CAMPAIGNING
### Jim Miller

Ambushed on the Santa Fe trail, Sean Callahan is saved by two Indian strangers. But there'll be more lead and arrows flying before the band join Kit Carson against the Comanches.

# GUNSLINGER'S RANGE
## Jackson Cole

Three escaped convicts are out for revenge. They won't rest until they put a bullet through the head of the dirty snake who locked them behind bars.

# RUSTLER'S TRAIL
## Lee Floren

Jim Carlin knew he would have to stand up and fight because he had staked his claim right in the middle of Big Ike Outland's best grass.

# THE TRUTH ABOUT SNAKE RIDGE
## Marshall Grover

The troubleshooters came to San Cristobal to help the needy. For Larry and Stretch the turmoil began with a brawl and then an ambush.

## WOLF DOG RANGE
### Lee Floren

Will Ardery would stop at nothing, unless something stopped him first — like a bullet from Pete Manly's gun.

## DEVIL'S DINERO
### Marshall Grover

Plagued by remorse, a rich old reprobate hired the Texas Trouble-shooters to deliver a fortune in greenbacks to each of his victims.

## GUNS OF FURY
### Ernest Haycox

Dane Starr, alias Dan Smith, wanted to close the door on his past and hang up his guns, but people wouldn't let him.

## DONOVAN
### Elmer Kelton

Donovan was supposed to be dead. Uncle Joe Vickers had fired off both barrels of a shotgun into the vicious outlaw's face as he was escaping from jail. Now Uncle Joe had been shot — in just the same way.

## CODE OF THE GUN
### Gordon D. Shirreffs

MacLean came riding home, with saddle tramp written all over him, but sewn in his shirt-lining was an Arizona Ranger's star.

## GAMBLER'S GUN LUCK
### Brett Austen

Gamblers seldom live long. Parker was a hell of a gambler. It was his life — or his death . . .

## ORPHAN'S PREFERRED
### Jim Miller

Sean Callahan answers the call of the Pony Express and fights Indians and outlaws to get the mail through.

## DAY OF THE BUZZARD
### T. V. Olsen

All Val Penmark cared about was getting the men who killed his wife.

## THE MANHUNTER
### Gordon D. Shirreffs

Lee Kershaw knew that every Rurale in the territory was on the lookout for him. But the offer of $5,000 in gold to find five small pieces of leather was too good to turn down.

## RIFLES ON THE RANGE
### Lee Floren

Doc Mike and the farmer stood there alone between Smith and Watson. There was this moment of stillness, and then the roar would start. And somebody would die . . .

## HARTIGAN
### Marshall Grover

Hartigan had come to Cornerstone to die. He chose the time and the place, and Main Street became a battlefield.

## SUNDANCE: OVERKILL
### John Benteen

When a wealthy banker's daughter was kidnapped by the Cheyenne, he offered Sundance $10,000 to rescue the girl.